FRIENDS

Sophie looked concerned. "Dana, you seem so down. What is it? Is something wrong between you and Michael?"

I nodded, feeling the tears spring to my eyes. I blinked them back.

"Oh, Dana," said Carla. "Did he break up with you?"

"Not yet," I said, choking back a little sob. "I'm not sure exactly what's going on. All I know is that Michael is acting totally different toward me. When I saw him today in school he hardly said anything to me at all. He hasn't called, and I haven't got the nerve to call him. At the lake . . ."

"But this isn't the lake," Carla cut me off. "You're back in Greenfield now, and things are different. We're going to have such a good time this weekend, you're going to forget all about Michael. It'll be great fun. You'll see."

I managed a smile. I only hoped it was true.

Other **HIS AND HERS** *Books*
by B. B. Calhoun
from Avon Flare

NEW IN TOWN

His and

Hers

SUMMER DREAMS

B. B. CALHOUN

AN AVON  FLARE BOOK

This is a work of fiction. Names, characters, places, and incidents either are the product of the author's imagination or are used fictitiously. Any resemblance to actual events, locales, organizations, or persons, living or dead, is entirely coincidental and beyond the intent of either the author or the publisher.

AVON BOOKS
A division of
The Hearst Corporation
1350 Avenue of the Americas
New York, New York 10019

Copyright © 1998 by Christina Lowenstein
Published by arrangement with the author
Visit our website at http://AvonBooks.com
Library of Congress Catalog Card Number: 97-93866
ISBN: 0-380-78471-8

First Avon Flare Printing: January 1998

AVON FLARE TRADEMARK REG. U.S. PAT. OFF. AND IN OTHER COUNTRIES, MARCA REGISTRADA, HECHO EN U.S.A.

Printed in the U.S.A.

WCD   10 9 8 7 6 5 4 3 2 1

Chapter 1

Dana

I picked up the whistle that hung around my neck, put it to my lips, and blew hard.

"Stay on this side of the rope, please!" I called out, cupping my hand to my mouth.

The group of three younger boys who'd ducked under the rope that divided the deep part of the lake from the shallow area paddled quickly back toward the shore. I squinted. One of those kids looked awfully familiar. I put up my hand to shade my eyes from the early afternoon sun.

Sure enough, there was my little brother, Arnie. He spotted me gazing at him and waved back enthusiastically, a big grin on his face. He climbed out of the water and came trotting across the sand toward where I was sitting on the lifeguard stand.

"Hi, Dana!" he said, staring up at me.

I shook my head, softening a little. "Hi, Arnie."

1

"Did you see how far out I can swim?" he asked proudly.

"Yes, I did, Arnie," I said. "But you know you're not supposed to go past those ropes."

He glanced back toward the water, as if he'd just noticed the ropes.

"Oh," he said. "Right." He paused. "You mean even if my sister's the lifeguard?"

"*Especially* if your sister's the lifeguard," I said firmly. After all, if I couldn't get my own little brother to listen to me, how was I supposed to get anyone *else* at the lake to listen to me?

Arnie looked disappointed. Then, after a moment, he brightened. "Can I climb up there with you, Dana?"

I hesitated. Only guards were allowed up on the stand during beach hours. True, it *was* the last weekend of the summer, but still, I wanted to make sure Mr. Greeley, the beach supervisor, gave me my job back next year. And I'd already been in enough trouble with him lately.

"Sorry, Arn," I said sympathetically. "I can't. Maybe tonight at the barbecue, though. Beach hours will be over then."

"Okay, Dana," said Arnie. "Hey, you want to see me do a cannonball off the float?"

"Sure, go ahead," I said, as he ran off toward the water. "Just remember to stay inside the ropes!" I called after him.

I watched Arnie and the other kids playing in the

water and smiled. I was really happy that my mom and her new husband, Jeff, had brought Arnie and me to North Harbor for the summer, and that Jeff had managed to get me a job as a lifeguard at the lake. North Harbor was only a couple of hours away from where we lived in Greenfield, which is just outside of Chicago, but staying there was totally different.

The houses at North Harbor were all near the lake, so people were always at the beach. There were all these pretty pine trees around, and at night everything was quiet except for the crickets. Mom said that Jeff used to come here when he was a little boy, and that he had really wanted to come back. I could see why he liked it so much. I'd loved spending this summer at the lake house. In fact, it had probably been the best summer of my life.

Suddenly, my thoughts were interrupted when a towel landed on my head and covered my face.

"Hey!" I cried. I struggled to pull it off, but a pair of strong arms wrapped themselves around my shoulders from behind, trapping me. I started to laugh. I had a pretty good idea of who it was.

"Come on!" I yelled, still laughing, my voice muffled by the thick, red towel. "Let me out!"

The arms loosened their grip and the towel disappeared. I whipped around and saw Michael standing directly behind me, balanced on the top rung of the lifeguard stand. His curly, dirty-blond hair was a tangled mess cascading down to his collarbone, and he had a huge grin on his face. He looked great.

"Michael," I scolded gently, "you really shouldn't cover my eyes when I'm supposed to be watching the water, you know."

Michael climbed up and sat beside me.

"Don't worry," he said, tossing the towel over his shoulders, "I had my eye on the lake. Everything was okay." He leaned over to give me a quick kiss on the cheek.

I smiled. Michael Tyler was one of the main reasons that this had been such a good summer for me. Michael and I had actually gone to the same school, Williams Junior High, the year before, but we'd never really known each other. I mean, I'd noticed him in the halls and stuff, and I knew he was on the football team, but it was a pretty big school, and we didn't have any of the same friends. I might never have met him at all if he hadn't been at North Harbor for the summer.

It turned out that Michael's parents had a house at the lake, and that he had a job lifeguarding at the beach, too. In fact, three days a week his shift came right after mine, so I got to see him a lot. He used to come early so he could swim laps, and I used to watch him from the lifeguard stand. I couldn't help it, really. With his strong, tanned arms cutting through the water, he looked amazing. Then, afterward, when he'd show up for his shift, we'd usually say "hi" or something, but that was about it for a while.

Until the Fourth of July, that is. There were these fireworks over the lake, and Michael and I ended up sitting on a blanket on the beach with this other guard, Keith, his girlfriend, Suzanne, and her sister, Amy. We all talked and stuff, and I guess that kind of broke the ice between Michael and me. Anyway, he started showing up even earlier for his shifts whenever I was working, and we'd sit up on the guard stand together for a while after he'd swum his laps. Eventually we started hanging around together during our time off, too, riding our bikes, taking walks in the woods, and going down to the North Harbor General Store for ice cream.

Then, one day, just as I was about to dig into my double-fudge-walnut cone, Michael leaned over and kissed me. Since then, we'd spent just about every day together. And in two days, we'd be back home in Greenfield starting our first year at Hyde High School together.

Michael nudged me with his elbow. "Hey, Dana, what are you thinking about?"

I shrugged. "School."

"Yeah," Michael sighed. "In just a few days I'll have to be ready to show Coach Newman that I'm in good enough shape for the team."

"Oh, Michael," I said. "You're in incredible shape, you know that."

Michael exercised more than anyone I'd ever known. He was always swimming or riding his bike or something. And it showed, too. He was slim, but really strong. In fact, he could pick me up with just one arm.

"Besides," I added, "you were one of the best players in school last year, weren't you?"

"Dana, that was *junior* high," he answered. "This year we're talking about high-school football. Even for junior varsity, it's a whole other level."

I shrugged. I really didn't know anything about football. In fact, I'd never even *been* to a football game.

"I'm sure you'll be great," I assured Michael.

Just then, I spotted the green truck of the park supervisor pulling up in the parking lot.

Michael saw it, too. "Greeley's here," he said under his breath.

Mr. Greeley had this thing about Michael and me. He hated it when we sat on the guard stand together. Which wasn't fair, if you think about it. I mean, technically, the rules said that only guards were allowed to sit up there during beach hours. And Michael and I *were* both guards. Still, I wasn't about to argue. Like I said, it was the end of the summer, and I planned to renew my lifeguard certification and get my job back next year.

I turned to Michael.

"You'd better get going," I said quickly. "Or I'd better. What time is it? Whose shift is it now?"

"Mine, I think," he answered. "You go ahead."

He gave me another quick kiss, and I hopped down from the stand. He grinned and waved.

"Bye," I said.

"See you tonight, right?" he answered.

"Tonight? Oh, right, the barbecue. Okay," I said. "See you."

I spotted Mr. Greeley getting out of his truck. With another quick wave to Michael, I headed off across the sand in the opposite direction, toward the dirt road that led to our house.

Back at the house, I found my mother and Jeff in the kitchen making sandwiches. Seeing them huddled together over the kitchen counter made me smile. I was really happy for my mom. She and my dad had divorced when I was seven. After seeing her on her own with just me and Arnie for so long, it was nice to see my mom with someone who really cared about her.

Jeff was in his swim trunks, and my mom was wearing an oversized blue-and-white-striped T-shirt over her bathing suit.

"Hi, Dana," she said, looking up at me with a smile. "We were just going to take these down to the beach. Did you see your brother down there?"

I nodded. "He's playing with a bunch of kids." I peered at the sandwiches. "What kind?"

"Tuna and egg salad," Jeff answered. "You want to come back down with us for lunch?"

I shook my head. "I really need to take a shower. Leave me a tuna, though, okay?"

"Sure," said my mother. "Oh, by the way, you got some mail. I left it in your room for you."

"Thanks, Mom," I called back. "See you guys later."

I found the letter on the dresser in my room. I picked it up excitedly. The return address said *Grado Bajo, Puerto Rico*, so I knew right away that it was from Carla, and that there would probably be a letter in there from Sophie, too. Carla Meléndez and Sophie Garth were my two best friends. Since I was spending the summer at North Harbor while Carla visited her cousins in Puerto Rico, and Sophie had a job as a counselor at a day camp in Greenfield, Carla had come up with this really great system for us all to keep in touch. See, first, I sent a letter to Sophie in Greenfield, and then Sophie added her own letter to it and sent them off to Carla in Puerto Rico. Then Carla took out my letter and put in one of her own before sending the package back to me. When I got it, I was supposed to read it, add my own letter, and take out Sophie's. This way we were able to tell each other about our summers and keep up with everything. We'd passed the letter packs around a few times already, and it had worked out great.

I held the envelope in my hand for a moment. I was dying to read it right away, but I also felt hot and sandy. Besides, it would be more fun to read it when I could sit down and take in every single word. I decided to save the letter and hop in the shower first. I put the letter back on my dresser, grabbed a towel from the hook on the back of my door, and headed outside.

One of my favorite things about the lake house was the outdoor shower. It was attached to the back of the house, and was surrounded by a high wooden fence, so it was private, but the top of it was open, so you could see the sky and the tops of the trees. It felt amazing showering in the woods like that. I wished I could do it all the time.

A few minutes later, my hair was wrapped in a towel, and I was dressed in my cut-off shorts and a faded old red sweatshirt of Michael's that said *Hyde Hornets*. I grabbed the letter from my dresser and went down to the kitchen to pour myself some iced tea and pick up the sandwich my mom and Jeff had left for me. Then I headed toward the screened-in back porch and sat down on the daybed there.

I tore open the envelope, took a bite of my sandwich, and began to read. As I expected, the first letter was from Sophie. I recognized her wild, curlicued writing right away.

Hi Everybody—

Wow, I can't believe there are only two and a half weeks left of summer. And then we'll be actual <u>high school students!</u> YIKES! Actually, I'm totally, incredibly excited. And, of course,

I'm dying to know what play the Drama Club's doing. We're all still joining, right?

Sophie and Carla and I had agreed to try out for the Drama Club production this year. Sophie really wants to be an actress, and Carla's sure she's going to be a playwright someday, so she says it's good for her to get as much experience as she can with different plays. I might want to be an actress, too. I'm not sure yet. But I've always loved being in plays.

The little drama group I started at camp is doing their play next week, and we're inviting all their parents and all the camp counselors and everyone. I think they're going to be great—they're sooooo cute! (Although getting them to memorize their lines wasn't easy, believe me.) Ms. Rohan, the head of the camp, says she's so pleased with what I've been doing that she wants to make the drama group a permanent thing there every summer. Isn't that incredibly cool?

Dana, that story in your last letter about you and Michael and the ice-cream-cone kiss sounded incredibly romantic (and a little sticky, too!). I'm so happy for you. I don't know Michael at all, but he's definitely cute, and I'm sure he must be really nice, too.

I smiled. I'd been writing Sophie and Carla about Michael all summer, and my last letter had been about how he'd kissed me near the general store. But that kiss seemed so long ago now. Michael and I had spent practically every day together since then.

Speaking of guy stuff, how's everything going with Pedro, Carla? I'm keeping my fingers crossed for you. Well, I guess this will probably be my last letter, since by the time it gets to Carla and then to Dana the summer will be practically over. I can't wait until both of you guys get back here. Greenfield seems totally empty without you!

Love,
Sophie

I sighed. Reading Sophie's letter almost made me feel like I *was* back in Greenfield, listening to her cheerful, excited voice. I couldn't wait to see her and Carla.

I took a sip of my iced tea and flipped to the next page to read Carla's letter. As usual, it was printed in neat block letters on lined paper. Carla's incredibly organized, the kind of person teachers love. She even keeps her socks arranged by color in her sock drawer! I guess it figures that Carla was the one who came up with the system for the three of us to write letters to one another.

DEAR AMIGAS,

HI. RIGHT NOW I'M SITTING HERE ON MY COUS-INS' BACK PORCH, LOOKING OUT AT THE BEACH. THERE ARE ALL THESE DARK CLOUDS OUTSIDE, AND IT LOOKS LIKE IT'S GOING TO RAIN.

It was kind of neat to think that Carla had been sitting on her back porch when she wrote this, and that now I was reading it on *my* back porch.

IT WAS GREAT TO GET YOUR LETTERS. I WAS IN KIND OF A DOWN MOOD WHEN THEY CAME, AND IT DEFINITELY CHEERED ME UP TO READ THEM. YOU SEE, PEDRO HAD JUST LEFT TO GO BACK TO SCHOOL IN SAN JUAN, AND I GUESS I WAS PRETTY DISAPPOINTED THAT NOTHING HAD HAPPENED BE-TWEEN US, AFTER ALL. HE'S CUTER THAN EVER, YOU GUYS, AND I REALLY HOPED WE'D FINALLY GET TOGETHER THIS SUMMER. BUT I THINK HE STILL SORT OF THINKS OF ME AS HIS FRIEND ESTEBAN'S

LITTLE COUSIN. WHICH IS RIDICULOUS, SINCE I'M <u>ONLY</u> TWO AND A HALF YEARS YOUNGER THAN HE IS!

Pedro is this guy in Puerto Rico that Carla has a huge crush on. She's known him ever since she was little, since he's her cousin Esteban's best friend, and Carla has been spending her summers with Esteban's family for practically her whole life.

WELL, I GUESS EVEN IF SOMETHING <u>HAD</u> HAPPENED WITH PEDRO, I STILL WOULD HAVE BEEN SAD THAT HE WAS GOING BACK TO SAN JUAN, RIGHT? DANA, YOU ARE SO INCREDIBLY LUCKY! IT SOUNDS LIKE YOU AND MICHAEL ARE HAVING A GREAT SUMMER. IT'S SUCH AN INCREDIBLE COINCIDENCE THAT YOU BOTH ENDED UP LIFEGUARDING THERE TOGETHER LIKE THAT. AND NOW YOU'LL GET TO START HIGH SCHOOL WITH A BOYFRIEND! THAT IS SO COOL.

SOPHIE, THAT STUFF YOU'VE BEEN DOING WITH THE DRAMA GROUP AT CAMP SOUNDS REALLY FUN. GOOD LUCK WITH YOUR PLAY—BREAK A LEG!!!

I MISS YOU GUYS, TOO. I CAN'T WAIT TO

GET BACK TO GREENFIELD AND HEAR ALL ABOUT
SOPHIE'S KIDS' BIG PERFORMANCE AND DANA'S
LOVE LIFE!

SEE YOU BOTH SOON.
LOVE,
CARLA

I put down the letter and thought about what Carla
had said—how in two days, I'd be a high school girl
with a boyfriend. I'd never really thought about it
that way before. I sounded so cool. And, of course,
it would be great to be back with my best friends,
too.

My stomach fluttered a little with excitement. It
had been a great summer, and it looked like things
were just getting better and better for me!

Chapter 2

Michael

I stepped out of the shower, and there was a loud knock on the other side of the bathroom door.

"Michael, let's get a move on in there!" called my father's voice. "There are other people waiting to use the bathroom in this house, you know."

"*Okay*, Dad," I answered. I wrapped a towel around my waist and quickly dried my hair with another one. Tossing the second towel around my shoulders, I opened the door.

I headed down the hall, passing my parents' room. There was an open suitcase lying on the bed, and my mother was folding clothes and carefully laying them into it. We were leaving to go back to Greenfield that night, and my mom was getting things ready.

Summer vacation technically still had one day left, tomorrow, but my father was making us leave right after the barbecue at the beach tonight, so we wouldn't run into traffic. My father has this thing about traffic. For my whole life, he's always made us leave for trips at weird times and take back roads and stuff just so there won't be lots of other cars.

My father came in from the living room as I continued toward my bedroom. He was wearing his terrycloth robe, and he had a towel over one arm.

He squinted at me. "Michael, when are you going to get a haircut?"

"Uh, I don't know," I began. I put my hand up to my damp hair. "I mean, it seems okay to me."

"Well, it won't seem okay to Rocky Newman, I can promise you that," he told me. My father and Coach Newman, the junior varsity football coach at Hyde High School, had played football together in college. "You just ask Matt. When Matt played for the J.V. Hornets, he always made sure to keep his hair trimmed short," my father went on. "Did it for the varsity team, too."

Matt's my older brother. He played for the junior varsity Hyde Hornets and then for the varsity team until last year, when he graduated. He'd spent the summer at a special football training camp, and now he was on his way to college, where he was going to play for my dad's and Coach Newman's old team.

I ran my fingers through my hair. "Well, I *guess* I could . . ."

"Good grooming," my father interrupted emphatically. "It shows respect. Coaches like that. You take it from me." He gave me a pat on the back and headed into the bathroom.

"Okay, Dad, sure," I said, continuing toward my room.

I supposed it wasn't that big a deal whether or not I got a haircut. And if going to the barber would actually help me get a spot on the team, I was definitely willing to do it.

"Make sure you've got everything of yours packed up and ready to go before you head for that barbecue, son!" my father called after me. "I want to leave here at ten o'clock sharp."

"Okay, okay," I answered, shutting my door.

I glanced out the window at the sky, which was growing darker. I knew Dana was probably already down at the beach, so I hurriedly pulled on some jeans and an old blue T-shirt. It was funny about Dana—even though I'd just seen her that afternoon, I was really looking forward to being with her again. We'd spent a lot of time together lately, and I guess I'd kind of gotten used to it. It was strange to think that we'd gone to the same school but hadn't even talked to each other before this summer.

I ran a comb through my hair and stuffed my feet into my sneakers. On my way out of the house, I found my mother in the kitchen, packing up food from the refrigerator.

"Hey, Mom, are you and Dad going to come down to the beach?" I asked her.

"Oh, I'll probably pop down for a spell," she

answered with a little sigh, "but I've got a few more things to do here first. I'd like to get your father to come down for a while, too, but he'll want to start loading up the car right away."

"Well, maybe you can talk him into a quick burger or something," I said. "If it won't mess up his schedule too much."

She smiled. "Maybe. You go on ahead and have fun, though, Michael." She reached out and gave my arm a little squeeze. "It's the last few hours of summer. You enjoy them."

The last few hours of summer, I thought as I headed outside and made my way down the dirt path through the woods to the beach. Normally, thinking about the summer ending wouldn't make me too happy. Summer was the best time of the year, and this summer had definitely been a good one. But this year I was kind of looking forward to the fall. For one thing, I'd finally have my chance to try to prove myself as a Hyde Hornet. I'd been waiting for that ever since I'd seen Matt play his first game with the junior varsity team four years ago.

A few moments later, I arrived at the beach. The sun was setting behind the trees, and the lake was sort of glowing. It looked nice. There was a long line of picnic tables piled high with food, and a big barbecue set up near one end, covered with sizzling hot dogs, hamburgers, and chicken.

Keith Strand, another of the lifeguards at the lake,

walked over to me. Balanced on his hands were two paper plates filled with food.

"Hey, Michael," he said with a grin. "Looking for Dana?"

"Yeah, have you seen her?" I asked.

Keith nodded toward the water. "She's over there with Suzanne."

I looked and saw Dana and Suzanne, Keith's girl-friend, standing by the lake. Suzanne was talking, and Dana was leaning toward her and listening, nodding every once in a while. As usual, Dana looked great. She's one of those girls who can make cut-offs and a faded sweatshirt look pretty.

As I walked toward her, I realized that it was *my* sweatshirt she had on. Actually, it was my brother Matt's, originally, but he had handed it down to me when it got too small for him. And I had lent it to Dana one night when we were skipping rocks at the lake and it got chilly. I grinned. I liked seeing her in my shirt.

Keith and I walked over to the girls, and Keith handed Suzanne one of the plates he was holding. I put my arm around Dana's shoulder and she turned her head to give me a quick kiss.

"Hi," she said, quickly tucking a lock of her straight, smooth, blonde hair behind one ear.

"Hi," I answered, kissing her back. "Nice sweat-shirt."

She laughed.

"Hi, Michael. Are you just getting here?" asked Suzanne.

I nodded. "Yeah, well, I ran a couple of miles after my shift ended, and then I had to help my parents pack up the house," I explained.

"Oh, that's right, you guys are leaving tonight, aren't you?" asked Keith, munching on a chicken leg.

"Yeah, my dad has this thing about beating the traffic," I said. "In fact, we're supposed to leave at ten, right after the barbecue."

"Your family's not going back until tomorrow, though, right, Dana?" asked Suzanne.

Dana nodded. "Actually, I have one more shift at the beach tomorrow morning, so I guess we'll go sometime after that."

"Afternoon, huh? *Peak* traffic time, my father would say. You'd better watch out," I joked.

"Yeah, well, I hope we make it okay," Dana joked back.

Suzanne laughed. "Seriously, though, it's so great for you guys that you're both going back to the same place. You know, that you'll be back together in another day."

"That's right," said Keith. "You two are pretty lucky that you both live in Greenfield and even go to the same school."

He put his free arm around Suzanne, and she looked a little sad. Keith's from Chicago, but Suzanne's from someplace in Indiana, several hours away. They obviously weren't going to be seeing too much of each other after tomorrow.

"But you guys are still going to try to visit each other sometimes, right?" asked Dana. "And you can always write to each other and stuff."

"Yeah, I guess," Suzanne managed. But she still looked pretty upset.

"Hey," said Keith, trying to sound cheerful, "have you guys tried this chicken yet? It's really good."

"Yeah," added Suzanne enthusiastically. "Mrs. Burdock, who has the house next to ours, made the barbecue sauce. My dad always tries to get the recipe from her, but it's some kind of secret formula or something."

"Whatever it is, it's great," said Keith, licking his fingers.

"Well, I guess we'd better go try some," I said.

"Definitely," Dana agreed with a nod. She turned to Keith and Suzanne. "Catch you guys later."

"Yeah, see you," I added.

I took Dana's hand, and we threaded our way through the groups of people who were eating and talking on the sand. When we got to the tables, we served ourselves some food. I took two chicken legs, a hamburger, potato salad, and two ears of corn. We found some space to sit on a log under some trees, and I noticed Dana staring at the big pile of food on my plate.

"Time to start bulking up a little," I explained.

"Bulking up?" she repeated.

"Sure," I said. "The season will be starting soon. I have to try to put on a few extra pounds."

"The season?" Dana said, looking perplexed. "Oh, you mean football! You're kidding, you're really supposed to get heavier for that? But you look fine the way you are."

"I may *look* fine, but I'm not going to *play* fine unless I gain about seven pounds," I explained.

"Oh," said Dana softly.

I glanced at her as she took a bite of her potato salad. I couldn't help thinking she looked a little disappointed. It seemed weird, though. I mean, even if she *did* like the way I looked now, what was the big deal about a few extra pounds—especially if it meant I'd play better?

Suddenly, a bunch of little kids and a dog went racing past us, kicking up sand behind them and knocking into Dana. I recognized one of the kids as Arnie, Dana's little brother. Arnie's cute, but he's a bit of a troublemaker sometimes. I was always having to yell at him to stay on the right side of the ropes when I was lifeguarding.

"Ugh!" said Dana, looking down at the ground.

I glanced down and saw that her ear of corn was lying in the sand.

"Here, take one of mine," I said, handing her one from my plate.

"Thanks," she said. She shook her head. "*Noth-*

ing's safe around Hurricane Arnie these days. Boy, I feel sorry for his teacher this year.''

"He's going into fifth, right?" I asked. "At Ellis Elementary? Who does he have?''

"I think my mom said his teacher's name is Mrs. Fletcher," said Dana.

"Oh, yeah?" I said. "Mrs. Fletcher was my fifth-grade teacher, too.''

"You're kidding!" said Dana. "You went to Ellis Elementary?''

"Of course," I told her. "Where'd you go?''

"Lincoln," she answered. "We didn't move near Ellis and Williams until I was in seventh grade.''

I looked at her a moment. It was funny how little I really knew about Dana—outside of stuff that had happened at the lake this summer, that is. I mean, sure, we'd spent a lot of time together during the past month, but being at North Harbor was sort of like stepping out of our *real* lives for a couple of months, if you thought about it. At North Harbor there was no football, no school, nothing but hanging around and having fun together.

I looked at the lake—the deep blue sky that was getting darker, the kids running around, Dana chewing happily on her corn—and I thought again about what my mother had said, that these were the last few hours of summer. For the first time, I began to wonder exactly what it was going to be like to be back in Greenfield, back in *real* life again.

Chapter 3

Dana

"Okay, Dana, let's have that bag," Jeff said.

I lugged my big green duffle bag across the driveway and dropped it by the back of the car with a thud. Jeff lifted it, grunting a little, and heaved it into the station wagon.

"What do you have in there, Dana, bricks?" he said.

"Just clothes," I answered with a laugh.

The truth was, most of the clothes in that bag I hadn't even worn all summer. When my mom and Jeff had said we were coming to North Harbor, I'd packed all my favorite summer outfits—long, flowered skirts, peasant blouses, and floppy straw hats—but somehow once I got there, I ended up wearing T-shirts and jeans or cut-offs every day. North Harbor was like that, really casual. Nobody *ever* dressed up. The amazing thing was, I ended up liking it that way. I mean, sure, I'll always love putting together cool outfits, but it was also pretty nice not having to think about what I put on all summer. Besides, all those long skirts and floppy hats I brought probably wouldn't have been too practical for all the bike riding and hiking and stuff Michael and I ended up doing together.

My mother came out of the house, letting the screen door bang behind her. In her hands was a red plastic cooler.

Jeff smiled at her. "Almost all packed up, Louisa."

"Good," she said, smiling back at him. "I fixed us some snacks for the road. I guess we should get moving soon. Now, if we could only find Arnie. Does anyone know where he went?"

"He's probably down at the lake. I'll go get him," I volunteered.

"Thanks, Dana," said my mother.

As I made my way down the dirt road that led to the beach, I couldn't help feeling kind of funny. For one thing, I was wearing sneakers and socks for the first time in months. But it was more than that. It just felt weird knowing I was walking down to the lake for the last time that summer, and thinking about the fact that Michael's family was already gone, back in Greenfield.

I had so many great memories from the lake and North Harbor—sitting in the sand, watching the fireworks and talking to Michael for the first time, hanging out with him on the lifeguard stand at the end of my shift while we watched out for Mr. Greeley, walking in the woods, bike riding, the barbecue last night. I couldn't help feeling a little sad that the summer was ending.

But, I reminded myself, it's not like things are *really* ending. Even though we wouldn't be at the lake anymore, Michael and I would still be seeing each other every day in school. And we could spend lots of time together after school and on the weekends, too. In fact, I might even be able to see him in just a couple of hours, when I got back to Greenfield. Besides, leaving North Harbor meant I'd be able to be with Sophie and Carla again, I thought excitedly. Maybe all four of us could even do some things together. I couldn't wait for them to get to know Michael.

I approached the lake and scanned the beach for Arnie. There weren't nearly as many people there as usual, since so many families had already left for home, and I spotted him pretty easily, playing in the sand behind the lifeguard stand with some other kids.

"Arnie!" I called.

He looked up at me and I gestured for him to come. He waved back at me.

I sighed. "Arnie!" I called again. "Come on! It's time to go."

He continued playing in the sand, and I trudged

across the beach toward him. Finally, when I reached the group, he looked up again.

"Oh, hi, Dana," he said.

I sighed again. "Arnie, come on. We have to go. We're driving back to Greenfield."

His face fell. "We are?"

I shook my head in amazement. How had he managed to forget something like that?

"Yes, we are," I said. "Remember? School starts tomorrow? Summer's over?"

"Oh, yeah. Okay, bye, you guys," he said to the other kids, standing up. "See you."

"See you, Arnie. Bye!" they called back as the two of us started across the sand together.

As we made our way up the dirt road toward the house, Arnie turned to me. "I had fun here, Dana," he said.

"Yeah, Arnie," I answered with a smile. "So did I."

Later that evening, Jeff, my mother, Arnie, and I finally finished dragging everything from the car into the house.

"Look at that, it's almost six o'clock already," said my mother, glancing at the hall clock in surprise.

"Well, that traffic we hit slowed us up a little," said Jeff.

I smiled, thinking of Michael, and what he'd said about his father and traffic. I wondered if Michael was home, what he was doing. Maybe I should give him a call or something.

"I'm hungry," Arnie complained.

"But, sweetie, you had two peanut butter and jelly sandwiches in the car," said my mother.

"So, I'm *still* hungry," said Arnie.

"Well, we have absolutely nothing in the house," said my mother, looking concerned.

"Actually, I'm kind of hungry, too," said Jeff. "How about if I go out and pick up a pizza for dinner?"

"That sounds like a good idea," said my mother.

"Pizza, yay!" said Arnie. "Can I come?"

"Sure," said Jeff. "What about you, Dana? Want to go with us?"

"Actually, I think I'll stay here. I kind of want to call Michael, if that's okay," I said.

"Are you sure he's home?" asked my mother. "A lot of people I talked to at the lake were leaving later in the day."

"Actually, his family left last night, after the barbecue," I explained. "His dad makes them go then, so they don't get stuck in traffic."

"Not a bad idea," said Jeff. He turned to Arnie. "Okay, come on. Let's go get that pizza before we both starve to death."

I grabbed hold of my duffel bag and pulled it down the hall and up the stairs. I opened the door to my room and looked around. It felt really weird to be back home after so long. Everything in my room looked the same, but also *different* somehow, in a way I couldn't explain. I guess it was just that I hadn't seen it in a couple of months. It was almost like I'd forgotten what my room looked like or something.

I sat down on the edge of my bed and fingered the tassels on the bedspread my grandmother had helped me crochet last year. The telephone was right in front of me, on the night table, but for some reason I didn't pick it up. I wanted to call Michael, but something felt strange about it.

Then I realized what it was. I had never called Michael at his house in Greenfield before. The truth was, I'd only called him a couple of times at the Tylers' place in North Harbor. People didn't seem to call each other much at the lake. I guess it was because everybody saw each other practically every day on the beach or in town. And Michael and I knew we'd always run into each other, so there'd never been any reason to call, really.

In fact, I suddenly realized, I didn't even *have* Michael's phone number in Greenfield! But I knew where I could find it. I stood up and walked over to my desk. Then I pulled last year's notebook off the shelf above the desk and searched through the back for the Williams Junior High eighth-grade class list.

There it was on the third page—"Michael Tyler; parents: John and Helen Tyler"—and their telephone number. I went back to my bed, picked up the phone, and dialed.

A woman answered. I didn't recognize her voice. It didn't sound like Michael's mother, but I wasn't sure since I'd only spoken to her a few times. Maybe it was one of his parents' friends or something.

"Um, hi," I said, suddenly feeling kind of funny. "Can I please speak to Michael?"

"Michael is not here," said the woman. "May I take a message?"

"No, that's okay," I answered quickly. Somehow I didn't feel comfortable leaving him a message. I'd just call back later, or maybe I'd wait for him to call me.

I couldn't help wondering where Michael was, though. It was kind of strange, not knowing. Not that he wasn't supposed to go out or anything. It was only that at North Harbor I pretty much knew where I could find him most of the time—on the beach during his shifts, jogging or working out afterwards, and mostly hanging out with me on his time off—and I realized that I'd grown used to it.

But before I could think about it anymore, the phone rang. Eagerly, I reached over to pick it up. Maybe it was Michael.

"Hello?" I said.

"Dana! Oh, my gosh! Hi!" It was Carla.

"*Carla?*" I practically squealed. "Hi! Where are you?"

"Where do you think? At home! Sophie's over here, too."

I heard Sophie lean into the phone. "Hi, Dana!"

she called. "Hurry up and get over here!"

"Can you?" asked Carla. She lowered her voice. "I mean, you don't have a date with Michael or anything, do you?"

"No, no," I answered quickly. A date with Michael, it sounded so funny. Even though we'd spent most of the last month together, I'd never actually had a real *date* with Michael.

"Well, then, come on," said Carla. "My mom said you and Sophie can eat here if you want."

"I'll ask my mother," I said. "I'm sure it's okay, though. We're just having pizza here."

"Okay, see you soon," said Carla happily.

Two hours later, Sophie, Carla, and I were sitting in Carla's room together. Carla was perched backward on her wooden desk chair, and I sat on the edge of her bed. Sophie sat on a pillow on the floor, cross-legged, twirling a lock of her long, curly, reddish-brown hair in her fingers.

"Whew, I'm stuffed," said Sophie. "Your mom's chicken is so incredibly good, Carla."

"And I love those fried banana things," I added.

"*Plátanos*," said Carla.

"What?" asked Sophie.

"*Plátanos*," Carla said again. "They're not bananas, they're plantains, *plátanos*."

"Well, whatever they are, they're yummy," Sophie agreed.

"We had them all the time in Puerto Rico," said

Carla. "There were plantains growing all over the place on my uncle's property. And mangoes and guavas, too. Every day I used to wake up and pick my own breakfast right outside my bedroom window. After I went for a swim—in the ocean, that is."

"Wow, that sounds really nice," I said.

"Yeah," Carla said, playing wistfully with the end of her long, thick, brown braid, "it would have been even nicer if Pedro had ever actually *noticed* me, though."

"Hey, don't complain," said Sophie. "Remember, while both of you guys were splashing around on the beach, I was sweltering here in the hot city all summer."

"But you had fun, too, Soph," I pointed out. "At least it sounded in your letters like you really liked working at that camp."

"Yeah, I did," Sophie admitted with a smile. "Those kids were so cute, and they did really well with their play, too. I was totally proud."

"And you must have a ton of money saved up now," said Carla.

"Saved?" Sophie repeated.

"From your job," said Carla. "I mean, you *did* work all summer, Sophie, didn't you?"

"Well, yeah," said Sophie with a little shrug. "But somehow the money didn't exactly get saved up."

"You mean you spent it all?" Carla asked, her eyes widening.

"What did you get?" I asked. I hadn't had a chance to spend my lifeguarding money on much yet, but I planned to buy a bunch of new CDs as soon as I could get down to the music store at the Greenfield Mall.

Sophie shrugged again. "I didn't get anything, really. Well, I mean, sure, I bought stuff. You know, sodas and snacks and things on my breaks from work. And I got a couple of pairs of cool earrings I saw at a store in the mall one day. Oh, yeah, and this other girl I worked with, Sara, and I went to the movies a couple of times . . ."

"You're *kidding*," Carla interrupted her. "You mean you just spent it all on *stuff*? You didn't save it, but you didn't buy anything important with it, either?" She shook her head. "I *never* could have done that."

Sophie grinned. "Actually, it was easy." Then her face lit up. "Oh, I did buy *one* kind of big thing, a dress. I found this great store near where I worked called 'Dream Again.' All the clothes were antique, you know, from the forties and fifties and sixties or whatever. Anyway, one day there was this totally incredible dress in the window. I knew I had to have it."

"What's it like?" I asked her.

Her eyes were shining. "Well, it's long, almost down to my ankles, and it's made up of all these different, really pretty scarves sewn together, so it's all flowy and stuff. The woman in the store said it was one-of-a-kind. I'll wear it to school tomorrow so you guys can see it.''

"It sounds perfect for you, Soph," I said.

And it did. Sophie was always putting together really creative outfits, stuff that would probably look crazy on anyone else, but that somehow looked great on her. This dress sounded just like something she would wear.

"It sounds pretty," agreed Carla. "And at least you bought *one* special thing with the money from your job, Sophie. I mean, if you weren't going to save it, that is."

"Yeah, I guess maybe I should have saved *some* of it, though," Sophie admitted. "I guess one nice dress isn't *that* much to end up with after a whole summer of working."

"Well, not compared to what *Dana* ended up with after *her* summer of work," joked Carla, raising her eyebrows at me.

"Huh?" I said. What was she talking about?

Sophie laughed. "Really. Maybe *I* should get a job as a lifeguard next year. I can't swim very well, but I bet I could learn pretty fast if a cute boyfriend came along with the job."

"Oh," I said, blushing as I realized what they were talking about. "You mean Michael."

"Of *course* we mean Michael," said Carla. She leaned toward me. "You haven't said a word about him, Dana. You haven't told us *anything*!" Then she looked concerned. "Everything's okay between you guys, isn't it?"

"He's still your boyfriend, right?" asked Sophie.

"Oh, yeah, of course," I answered quickly. Although it was starting to sound a little funny to hear them call him "my boyfriend" all the time like that. I mean, sure, I guessed it was true, but I'd never actually *called* Michael that, myself. At North Harbor Michael had just been . . . well, *Michael*.

"Well, then, tell us everything," said Sophie eagerly. "Last thing I heard, you guys were kissing over ice cream. What happened next? Did he ask you out on a date?"

I laughed a little. "Not exactly. I mean, it wasn't like that there. There wasn't really anywhere to *go* on dates."

"I don't get it," said Sophie. "So what did you guys do together?"

"Well," I said, remembering, "we hung around at the lake a lot. Sometimes he'd come early for his lifeguarding shift and we'd sit together and talk. And we went for a lot of bike rides."

They both looked at me, waiting for me to go on. But I didn't have much more to say. Somehow, it was hard to explain to my friends what the summer had been like for Michael and me.

"Oh," said Carla finally.

"It was really nice, you guys," I tried. "I mean, I know it sounds kind of boring when I talk about it, but in a way that's what was so nice about it.'' Then I thought of something. ''It was almost like the way the three of *us* hang around together, the way we don't actually have to *do* something or *go* somewhere to have fun.'' I glanced around the room. ''Kind of like this.''

''Only with sand and water,'' joked Sophie.

''Right,'' I said, laughing.

''That sounds great, Dana,'' Carla said sincerely. ''I know that's just how I would have wanted things to be between Pedro and me in Puerto Rico.'' She grinned. ''Actually, that's just how things *were*, lots of hanging around together and not doing much. Except that my cousin Esteban was always there, too. And there were *definitely* no kisses over ice cream.''

We all laughed.

''So when are you going to see Michael next?'' asked Carla.

''Yeah,'' said Sophie. ''And when do we get to meet him? You know, *really* meet him, I mean, now that he's your boyfriend.''

I paused. Michael and I hadn't actually made any definite plans. I guess we just weren't used to doing things that way, after how things had been in North Harbor. I didn't feel like telling my friends that I hadn't talked to him since I'd gotten home.

''Oh, I don't know,'' I said, shrugging a little. ''I mean, obviously, I'll see him in school tomorrow. I guess we'll talk about it then.''

Carla and Sophie exchanged brief glances. Then Carla cleared her throat.

"Okay, sure," said Sophie quickly. "Whatever you want, Dana. You're the one who knows how things are between you and Michael."

But somehow, I wondered if that were true. Sitting there in Carla's room, listening to Carla and Sophie talk about *dates*, and call Michael my *boyfriend*, everything suddenly started to seem really different from the way it had been in North Harbor. Now that we were back in Greenfield, now that there was no lake, no lifeguarding, and no bike rides, what exactly *were* things going to be like between Michael and me?

CHAPTER 4

Michael

I stood on the fifty-yard line of the Hyde High playing field, looking up at the empty bleachers. I jogged a few steps and took in a deep breath of the warm afternoon air. Tomorrow was the first day of school, so no one was around. But in a few short weeks, these seats would be filled with cheering fans dressed in Hornets red. I'd spent four years sitting in those bleachers, watching my brother Matt play first for the junior varsity and then for the varsity teams. And now I was finally going to get my chance to prove that I was good enough to play on this field, in a Hornets uniform. I couldn't believe it.

Suddenly, something went whizzing by my head. When it bounced on the ground a couple of yards in front of me, I realized it was a football.

"Hey!" called a voice. "You'd better work on those reflexes if you want to make the team."

I turned around and saw Bruce Eakin, a guy I recognized as the starting middle linebacker on the J.V. team.

"Oh," I said, feeling a little embarrassed. "I didn't see you there."

He nodded toward the ball. "Send it back this way."

I took a couple of steps, picked up the ball, and threw it back to him.

He raised his eyebrows. "Hey, not bad. You've got an arm there. You a freshman?"

I grinned. "As of tomorrow."

He threw me back the ball. "You play?" he asked.

I nodded. "I did last year, at Williams Junior." I tossed him the ball.

"You should go out for the J.V. team," said Bruce. "What's your name?"

"Michael Tyler," I answered.

"Tyler, huh?" He squinted at me. "Hey, wait a minute, are you Matt Tyler's little brother?"

"That's right," I answered.

He looked impressed. "Matt was an awesome fullback."

I grinned. "I play fullback, too."

He grinned back. "Coach Newman might be glad to hear that. If you play as well as your brother, that is," he said. "The J.V. team starts working out on Thursday, you know. You should come, show the coach what you've got. Maybe you'll make the cut."

"I'll be there," I promised.

"Hey, Mike, a bunch of the guys from the team are going to hang out at Cal Harrison's place now. You want to come? We can play some pool in his basement, and I'll introduce you to everybody."

I paused a moment. I knew my parents were going out to dinner tonight, which meant it would only be me at home after Rose, the woman who comes to clean for us, left. But I had kind of been thinking I might see Dana. I wasn't even exactly sure when she'd be home from the lake, though. Besides, this seemed like a pretty good chance for me to get to know the guys on the Hornets. And Cal Harrison would be on the varsity team this year. Maybe that meant there would be some varsity players there, too. I could always call Dana later. And anyway, I knew I'd see her in school tomorrow.

"Okay, sure," I said to Bruce. "That sounds great."

Later that evening, I sat next to Bruce in the rec room in Cal Harrison's basement, watching Mark Rapetti take his shot. Mark was starting end on the J.V. Hornets, and he wasn't too bad a pool player, either. He had just won three straight games of eight ball.

He banked a ball into the side pocket with a combination shot, and sank his next three balls before he finally missed.

The next shot was Greg Stone's, the short, blond

safety on the varsity team. Greg tried to slice the ten ball into the corner pocket, but was way off and missed the ball entirely.

"What's the matter, Stone?" teased Mark. "You're not playing so well tonight. Can't you play without Kirsten cheering you on from the side?"

"Aw, shut up, Rapetti," Greg answered good-naturedly, picking up his pool cue and walking away from the table. He chalked his cue.

"Kirsten is Greg's girlfriend," Bruce explained to me. "You've probably seen her. She's the one with the long blond ponytail."

I looked at him, confused. How did Bruce expect me to know Greg's girlfriend? After all, she must be a high school girl, right? Besides, "the one with the long blond ponytail" wasn't a very good description. It could probably fit a whole lot of girls at the high school.

"How would I have seen her?" I asked him.

He looked surprised. "Cheering, of course. You know, at the games. You used to come and watch your brother play, didn't you?"

"Oh," I said, finally understanding. "Kirsten's a cheerleader."

"Sure," said Bruce. "Varsity. My girlfriend, Ashley, is on the J.V. squad. She's a redhead. Not the one with the short red hair, that's Denise. She used to be my girlfriend back when I was a freshman. Ashley's got the long, curly, red hair and the green eyes."

"Oh," I said.

I'd seen a bunch of the J.V. games, too, last year with my dad, but the truth was I hadn't really looked all *that* closely at the cheerleaders. You know, they were cute and everything in their short red-and-white skirts, but there also seemed to me to be something kind of silly about them, the way they were always hopping around and yelling. Besides, I'd been way too busy watching the games to look at anything else. That, and listening to my father beside me on the bleachers analyzing every one of Coach Newman's plays.

Still, I didn't want to seem rude or anything. "Yeah, I'm pretty sure I know who you mean," I fibbed to Bruce. Then I thought of something. "Do all the Hornets go out with cheerleaders?" My brother Matt hadn't had a girlfriend in senior year, but I remembered him going out with a few cheerleaders before that.

"Mostly," said Bruce, his eyes on the pool table. Then he turned to me and grinned. "Don't worry, Tyler, if you make the J.V. team we'll find you a cute J.V. cheerleader to go out with, too." He stood up. "My shot."

"That's not what I—" I started. But Bruce was busy taking his shot.

I watched him bend over the table, his pool cue in his hands, and I thought of Dana. Dana definitely wasn't the cheerleading type. She seemed more . . . I don't know, serious, or creative, or something. I wasn't sure what. All I knew was I couldn't see her hopping around on the sidelines wearing a short skirt and yelling and shaking pom-poms in the air. And I couldn't really imagine her being friends with anyone who did, either.

Not that any of that mattered. If I wanted to make it to the Hornets, the important thing was how well I played football, not who I went out with, right? In fact, it seemed to me that I ought to just keep Dana and football separate. The more I thought about it, the more it made sense. There was Dana and there was football, and they didn't have to have anything to do with each other, right?

Thinking about Dana made me wonder what she was up to, though, and if her family was back from the lake yet. I decided to give her a call. I asked Cal Harrison if I could use the phone, and he showed me to one in the family room next door to the rec room.

Then, as I picked up the phone, a really funny thing happened. I realized I didn't have Dana's number. Here I was supposedly going out with her, and I didn't even know her phone number here in Greenfield. I guessed I should have asked her for it at the lake, but I didn't think of it.

I supposed I could call information for the number. I knew her stepfather's name—Jeff. But Jeff what? Dana's last name was Bryant, but that wouldn't be her stepfather's name. Then I remembered—Fulton. I'd seen it painted on their mailbox one afternoon when we'd stopped by their house at the lake so Dana could get her bike. I remembered because the mailbox had a boat painted on it, and for some reason it made me think back to fourth grade, when we'd learned about Robert Fulton inventing the steamboat.

I got the number from directory assistance and dialed. After three rings, Dana's stepfather picked up.

"Hi, this is Michael," I said. "Is Dana around?"

"Hi, Michael," said Jeff. "No, she went out. I'm pretty sure she won't be back until later tonight."

"Oh," I said. So Dana was busy tonight. Somehow I hadn't expected her to be.

"Do you want me to give her a message?" asked Dana's stepfather.

"Um, I guess you can just tell her that I called," I said. "Tell her I'll see her in school tomorrow."

"Okay, will do," he answered. "Good-bye, Michael."

I hung up and went back to the other room. Now that I knew Dana was out, I was really glad I had decided to come with Bruce to play pool at Cal's tonight. Still, I couldn't help wondering where Dana was.

Chapter 5

Dana

I stood in front of my new locker at Hyde High, slipped off my flowered backpack, and adjusted the strap on my purple velvet overalls. I couldn't believe it: my first day as a high-school student was about to begin. There were kids all around me, talking and putting books away and slamming lockers shut. I recognized a few faces from Williams Junior High and waved to a couple of people.

I didn't see Michael anywhere, though. And for some reason, I had kind of a nervous feeling in my stomach when I thought about seeing him at school. It didn't make sense. I mean, I'd seen him every day at the lake and I'd never felt nervous. And he *had called* my house last night and left a message, I reminded myself. There really wasn't anything to feel nervous about at all.

Then I felt someone tap me on the shoulder. I whirled around, hoping it was Michael.

But it was Sophie.

"Well, Dana, what do you think?" she asked.

She was standing with her hands on her hips, and she was wearing a floppy pink-and-white-flowered hat with the brim turned up in the front. She had on the long flowy dress made out of scarves that she'd told Carla and me about last night. On her feet were a pair of brown granny boots that laced up the front.

"Oh, Soph, you look so cute," I said.

"Thanks," she said with a smile. "Do you like the dress?"

"I love it," I told her. "It's perfect for you." In fact, I couldn't imagine anyone else in it. As I said, Sophie has a pretty unusual way of dressing sometimes, but she always looks really good in whatever she's wearing.

"Good," she said with a satisfied sigh. She rolled her eyes. "You should have heard my brother talking about it this morning. He said I looked like I had stolen all the curtains from the windows in my grandmother's house and decided to wear them."

"That's mean," I said. Sophie's older brother, Simon, is always teasing her like that. "And it's not true," I added.

Sophie shrugged. "I don't care." She grinned. "Anyway, I've always thought my grandma had pretty good taste in curtains."

I laughed.

"Hey, listen," she said, looking serious, "did you see the poster?"

"What poster?" I asked.

"Down the hall. It's all about the Drama Club tryouts," she answered. "They're after school."

"You mean today? You're kidding," I said. "We have to go."

"I know," said Sophie. "And we have to tell Carla about it. Have you seen her yet?"

I shook my head. "Not yet."

Sophie's eyes widened. "Oh, my gosh, do you think she might actually be late?"

"No way," I answered.

Carla's the type who's never late for anything. In fact, she got this special award at the end of our last year at Williams Junior High for having a perfect attendance record and for being on time during all three years of school. I knew there was no way she'd be late on the first day of high school.

"I guess you're right, Dana," said Sophie. "She must be around here somewhere."

I laughed. "Knowing Carla, she's probably been at school since seven o'clock this morning. I bet she's off someplace organizing something."

Sophie laughed, too. "Yeah, maybe she's rearranging all the books in the library by color."

"Right," I said, "or maybe—"

But then I stopped. There, coming down the hall toward me, was Michael. He didn't seem to have seen me yet, and I watched him make his way through the crowd of kids.

He looked different, somehow, not the way he had always looked at the lake. I supposed it was his clothes. At the lake, I'd never seen him wear anything but T-shirts and jeans, or swim trunks, but now he had on a pair of red warm-up pants with a white stripe down the side. Over his white T-shirt was a hooded gray sweatshirt with a zipper up the front, and he was carrying a gym bag over his shoulder. He looked really . . . *athletic*, or something.

Sophie nudged me. "Hello? Hello? Earth to Dana? Are you still there, or what?"

"Oh, sorry, Soph," I said with a start. "Um, yeah. What was it you were saying?"

Sophie followed my gaze, turning her head.

"Ooh, look," she said excitedly, "there's Michael!"

"Yeah," I said softly. I wasn't really sure what to do. Michael still hadn't seen me, and if I didn't do anything, in a moment or two he would probably pass right by me.

"Dana, aren't you going to say hello to your own boyfriend?" Sophie said, her eyes widening. "Hey, come on, don't I get to meet him now?"

I took a deep breath. Why did I feel so weird about all this? It was dumb. Like Sophie had said, Michael was my *boyfriend*. Of *course* I should say hello and introduce her. I raised my hand to wave to him.

Then, just as I was about to call out his name, Michael turned his head and spotted me. He grinned and started walking toward me. I smiled back, relieved. He looked happy to see me.

"Hi," said Michael, coming over to where Sophie and I were standing by my locker.

"Hi," I said back. We looked at each other. He leaned toward me a little, and for a moment I thought he was going to kiss me, but he didn't. Instead, he glanced at Sophie and then back at me.

"Hi, Michael," Sophie said cheerfully. "I'm Sophie."

"Hi," said Michael with a nod. "Um, nice to meet you."

"Actually, we went to school together last year," Sophie said, twirling one of her curls on her finger. "I went to Williams Junior, too."

"I figured," said Michael. "I mean, you looked familiar . . ." his voice trailed off.

I tried to think of something to say, but my mind was completely blank. Why did this feel so strange? It had never been hard for me to talk to Michael before. Maybe it was because Sophie was there. But that was silly. Sophie was one of my best friends.

Just then I saw Carla walking toward us. She was dressed in a black miniskirt and a yellow top, and she was cradling a stack of notebooks in her arms. She grinned and gave me a little nod, and I waved back. Michael turned to see who I was waving at.

"Michael, this is Carla," I said as she arrived.

"Hi, Michael," said Carla, a little out of breath. "Hi, guys. Hey, did you see the poster? Drama Club today, right?"

"I know, isn't it great?" said Sophie.

"Wow, I thought I wouldn't make it back here in time for class," Carla went on breathlessly. "What time is it, anyway, can you see my watch for me? How long do we have until first period?" She leaned over, still clutching the notebooks, trying to show me her wrist.

Michael pushed up his sleeve. "It's five of nine."

I looked at him, a little surprised. I'd never seen him wear a watch before. Not that I cared. It was just . . . different. Like his clothes.

"Oh, good, we still have five minutes," said Carla. She shifted the books in her arms. "I want to make sure I get a copy of my schedule into each one of my notebooks."

"Oh, my gosh, we're supposed to have copies?" said Sophie, looking alarmed. "I only got one. Am I going to be in trouble or something?"

"We *all* got only one," explained Carla. "But I just went over to the office and asked for permission to use the copy machine so I could make a bunch more for myself. You see, I like to have one in each notebook, one in my locker, one to keep at home—"

"Wow," I said, laughing a little. "I can't believe it. Only *you* would think of that, Carla."

I glanced up at Michael with a smile, but he didn't seem to be listening. In fact, he was sort of staring over my shoulder, at something or someone down the hall.

I turned to see what he was looking at. A tall, built-up blond guy with one of those incredibly short haircuts waved. I didn't recognize him. He definitely looked older than us.

"Hey, Tyler!" the guy called out. "Over here!"

"Just a second, Bruce!" Michael answered. "Be right there!" He turned to me. "Listen, I'd better go." He gave my arm a quick squeeze. "Talk to you later, okay, Dana?"

"Um, sure, okay," I said, a little surprised.

Sophie, Carla, and I watched Michael make his way down the hall. The blond guy gave Michael a punch in the stomach and then threw an arm around his shoulder. They walked off together, talking.

"Michael seems really nice, Dana," Sophie said softly.

"Yeah, he does," echoed Carla. "I mean, from what I could tell."

I didn't know what to say. Seeing Michael and introducing him to my friends hadn't turned out the way I had thought it would, at all. Michael hadn't seemed very interested in talking to them, or to *me* for that matter. I mean, he hadn't exactly been *un*-friendly, but he hadn't really been very friendly, either. In fact, it almost seemed like he was happier to see that Bruce guy than he had been to see me.

I could tell my friends were trying to be nice to me, though, and I didn't want them to see that I was a little disappointed. I shook my hair into place and tried to smile.

"Yeah, Michael's really sweet," I said, trying to sound cheerful. I picked up my backpack and slammed my locker door shut. "Come on, you guys, we'd better get to class before we're late."

Later that day, I walked out of science, my last-period class, and headed toward my locker, where Sophie and Carla and I had agreed to meet before going to the theater for the Drama Club auditions.

As I approached my locker, I saw that Michael was standing in front of it. I had only seen Michael twice that day, in English class, and then a couple of hours later as he was leaving the cafeteria when I was on my way in for lunch. We hadn't really had a chance to talk much either time. But now he must have come to my locker to wait for me, I realized happily. My heart began to beat faster. I felt better than I had all day, almost the way I used to at the lake, when we would meet at the lifeguard stand at shift-changing time.

Michael turned and spotted me.

"Hi, Dana," he said with a smile.

"Hi, Michael," I answered him.

Quickly, he bent down and gave me a kiss on the cheek.

"So, uh, what are you doing?" he asked.

"Right now?" I said.

"Well, yeah," he answered. "I mean, now that school's out."

"Actually . . ." I began. But just then Carla and Sophie came rushing over.

"Come on, Dana," Sophie said, grabbing my arm. She glanced up at Michael. "Oh, hi, Michael." Then she turned back to me. "I'm so excited. Let's go."

"Hold on a second," I said, laughing. "I haven't even put my books away."

"Well, *hurry,*" Carla urged. "We have to get there right away. I talked to this girl who's a junior, and she told me that sometimes tons of kids show up for these auditions, and if you're not one of the first, it can take forever to get to your turn."

"Okay, okay, I'm coming," I promised. I turned quickly to Michael. "Sorry, I have to go." I pulled open my locker and dragged out my backpack. "You see, we're all going to these tryouts—"

"No problem," Michael said quickly, cutting me off. "Let's just talk on the phone later."

"Okay, sure," I said, rummaging through my books and papers. "That sounds good." I turned to him to say good-bye, but he was already gone, walking away from me down the hall.

That night I lay in bed, reading the script for the first play that the Drama Club would be doing. So far, I liked it a lot. It was kind of an old-fashioned story, about a really rich girl whose parents want her to marry this guy who's the son of their best friends, but she wants to go off and explore the world and stuff, instead. I really hoped I'd get to be in it.

Sophie and Carla had both said my audition had gone really well, so maybe I would be in it. Ms. Gruss, the drama teacher, had everybody take turns reading this scene from the play that's supposed to take place between the girl's parents. When my turn came, I was kind of nervous at first, but I forgot all about it once I started reading the lines. Then, when I finished, Ms. Gruss asked me to read something else, a scene where Amanda, the main character in the play, is telling the guy that she doesn't want to marry him. Carla said she thought it was a really good sign that Ms. Gruss had me read that scene. She and Sophie were both totally convinced that Ms. Gruss would pick me to play Amanda.

I wasn't so sure, though. After all, Ms. Gruss had had a couple of other girls read some of Amanda's lines, too. Besides, I was sure just about every girl in there wanted to be picked to play Amanda. Of course, I would love to be picked to play her, but mostly I just hoped I would make it into the play. But Ms. Gruss had said that anyone who didn't get a part in the play could still do other stuff, like lights and scenery. So I knew I could be in Drama Club one way or another.

But I'd know tomorrow whether I got the part. Ms. Gruss had promised to post the casting list outside the theater in the morning. It was the first place I planned to go when I got to school.

The funny thing was, even though the audition had gone well, and even though the play seemed pretty interesting so far, I was having trouble concentrating on the lines of the script in front of me as I sat in bed. I couldn't help it. My eyes kept shifting to the white telephone sitting silently beside me on my night table. Why hadn't he called?

I sighed. What was it Michael had said when we saw each other that afternoon before the auditions? "Talk to you later on the phone," or something like that, right? But it was after ten o'clock, and he still hadn't called. Or had he meant that I was supposed to call him? But if that's what he'd meant, why hadn't he said so? Besides, why would he specifically want *me* to call *him*? I mean, did it really make such a difference which one of us called the other?

Finally, I put my script down beside me on the bed and reached over to pick up the telephone receiver. After all, if it didn't matter which one of us made the call, it might as well be me, right? The important thing was that we were going to talk to each other, wasn't it? The junior-high class list was still on the night table, and I picked it up.

But halfway through dialing the number, I hung up. I just couldn't call him. Not after the way he'd acted so funny that morning with me and Sophie and Carla. And not after the way he'd rushed off with that blond guy like that—almost like he was *glad* to get away. True, Michael *had* waited for me by my locker after school, and then it had seemed like he wanted to see me, maybe spend the afternoon together or something. Maybe he was upset because I had rushed off to the tryouts. But that didn't seem like enough of a reason not to call me.

I put the class list and the script on the night table and switched off the lamp. I hated having to think about all this stuff. Suddenly it seemed like everything between Michael and me was so complicated.

Why couldn't everything be easy between us again? I thought as I rolled over in bed and pulled up the covers. Why couldn't things just be the way they were at the lake?

Chapter 6

Michael

"We've got a great morning out there, Greenfield. Almost like summer is still with us. Mild and sunny and—"

I rolled over in bed and swatted at the clock radio, my eyes still glued shut. I felt like I could hardly move. My whole body ached from my workout with Bruce Eakin and Greg Stone the day before.

I'd run into Bruce and Greg on my way out of school, and they'd told me they were on their way to the gym to lift some weights, so I decided to go with them. I knew I could use the workout, with the first junior varsity football practice coming up on Thursday. And if I made the team, the season would be starting pretty soon after that. Besides, I figured Bruce and Greg could kind of show me around the high school gym. Maybe Coach Newman would even be there. It would be good for him to see that

I was serious about getting in shape for tryouts.

Well, it turned out that Coach Newman wasn't around, but I was still glad I had gone with Bruce and Greg. Those guys were *monsters* in the weight room. It was definitely one of the toughest workouts I'd ever had. Afterward I felt great, though, like I was ready for anything.

That is, I felt great until I fell asleep on top of my bed at eight o'clock with all my clothes on. I guess all that exercise really exhausted me. By the time I woke up, it was after midnight, and everyone in the house was asleep. My mom had put an afghan over me, and I quickly threw it off, got undressed, climbed between the sheets, and fell into another deep sleep.

Now, as I struggled to wake up, feeling every muscle in my body ache, I remembered that I had ended up never talking to Dana the night before. I'd meant to call her after dinner, but I hadn't managed to do it before I fell asleep. She had probably called me, I realized, but I guessed my mom hadn't wanted to wake me up.

I pulled myself out of bed, grabbed my bathrobe, and headed to the bathroom to take a shower. A hot shower is always the best thing for sore muscles. Still, I thought as I passed Matt's room, which was plastered with Hornets banners, I supposed I was going to have to get used to tough workouts like the one yesterday if I wanted to make the team.

I knew it wouldn't be easy. Every freshman and

sophomore who hoped to make the junior varsity team would be there training with Bruce and the others on Thursday, and Coach Newman would be watching all of us to see who was good enough to make the Hornets. After practice there would be cuts, and after every practice session for the next two weeks more guys would be cut, until the names of the ones who'd made the team were finally announced. It made me kind of nervous to think about it.

Fifteen minutes later, I eased myself downstairs to the kitchen. I found my dad at the round table in the center of the room, reading the paper and drinking his morning coffee.

He looked up as I came in.

"Hello, son," he said.

"Hi, Dad," I answered, heading for the refrigerator. "Where's Mom?"

"Oh, she's still upstairs fussing with her hair," said my father. "She's got an important meeting today with some clients."

My mom's in real estate. She sells houses to people. That's how we got our house years ago, when I was still a baby. My mom was showing it to this other couple, and as she was taking them around the house, she decided *she* loved it, so she took my dad to see it and they decided to buy it. My dad likes to say that she did one of her best sales jobs on him. But I know he really likes our house a lot, too.

"Well, Michael, tell me, what's happening with

that haircut?'' said my father, raising his eyebrows.

I shrugged, took a carton of orange juice out of the refrigerator, and poured myself a glass.

"Son," said my father, folding his newspaper. "You are serious about making the team, aren't you?"

"Of course I am, Dad," I answered. "But come on, how important is it what my hair—"

"*Very* important," my father snapped. "Like I told you, good grooming shows that you're serious, respectful. Coaches like that."

"Okay, fine, sure, I'll do it," I answered. I didn't really care. It's easier to give in than it is to argue with my father about stuff like that. Besides, maybe he was right.

"Great," he responded. "I'll pick you up today after school."

"Huh?" I said.

"To take you over to Mack's," said my father. "What time do you get out?"

Mack's was the barbershop where my dad used to take Matt and me to get our hair cut when we were little. I hadn't been there in years, but my father still got his hair cut there.

"Three-fifteen," I answered. Then I thought of something. "Hey, did I get any calls last night?"

My father shook his head. He stood up and took his coffee cup to the sink. "Don't think so, son."

That was strange. So Dana hadn't called, after all? I decided to go upstairs and ask my mother, just to be sure. Maybe my dad just hadn't been the one to take the call.

I put down my empty juice glass and headed for the stairs.

"See you this afternoon," my father called after me. "Three-fifteen sharp, got that?"

"Right, Dad, okay," I answered, starting upstairs.

I found my mom in my parents' bedroom on the second floor, leaning over her dresser. She was peering into the mirror and putting on some earrings. She was wearing a blue jacket and skirt, and she smelled like roses.

"Good morning, Michael," she said, turning to face me with a smile. "You must have been awfully tired last night to fall asleep like that."

"Hi, Mom," I said. "Yeah, I was pretty beat. Hey, listen, did anyone call me last night?"

"Oh, yes, as a matter of fact, you did get a call," said my mother. "Thanks for reminding me, dear."

So I was right. It had been my mom who had answered the phone when Dana had called.

"Did you tell her I was asleep?" I asked.

"Her?" my mother repeated, looking confused.

"Dana," I said. "Dana called last night, right?"

"Oh, no, honey, it wasn't Dana," said my mother. "It was a boy. Bruce, he said his name was. Bruce Eakin. He said he'd see you in school today."

"Oh," I said. "Okay."

But I couldn't help being surprised. Dana and I

had said we'd talk last night. Why hadn't she called when she hadn't heard from me?

I headed back to my room, still thinking. What if Dana was one of those girls who thought the *guy* was supposed to do all the calling? I hoped not. I hated that stuff. It was so dumb. I mean, why should everything be up to the guy, especially if you were already going out?

But Dana didn't seem like the old-fashioned, prissy type. At least, she hadn't at the lake. But then again, we'd never really talked on the phone much there, because we saw each other all the time. One of the things I had really liked about her was that she was so open and casual. The best times I'd had with Dana that summer were when we were just hanging around together, not doing much of any-thing.

That's why it surprised me that she hadn't called. Actually, a bunch of things had surprised me about Dana lately. Like the way she'd acted yesterday in school—all distant and stuff, not really talking to me the way she used to. She even *looked* different now. During the summer, Dana had always worn casual stuff—T-shirts and jeans. But yesterday she'd had on some fancy-looking purple thing and a pair of dangly earrings. Not that she didn't look good, but another thing I'd liked about Dana was that she didn't *have* to dress up to look good.

Maybe it was her friends. She sure had been eager to run off with them after school. What was it they said they were all going to do, check out some Drama Club thing? I guess I shouldn't have been that surprised. Back at Williams Junior, the theater crowd had always seemed kind of snobby.

I couldn't help wondering if Dana was going to end up acting like that, too, now that we were back at school. I wasn't the kind of guy the Drama Club types usually went out with, I knew that. At least in junior high, Drama Club people and football people didn't usually mix too much. I didn't see why that should make any difference, though—why who we were friends with had to have anything to do with Dana and me. But maybe Dana's friends didn't think she should be going out with me, or something.

Or could it be that Dana was starting to think that herself? I wondered.

Later that morning, as I was on my way to my Spanish class, I saw Dana headed down the hall toward me.

"Hi," I said, as we got closer.

"Hi," she answered.

We paused a few feet away from each other. Dana looked me quickly in the eyes and then looked away. I cleared my throat. I was about to say something about having fallen asleep before I could call her, but I stopped myself. I was actually kind of wondering what *she* would have to say about the night before, about why *she* hadn't called *me*, either. Did she even remember that we were supposed to talk?

"So," she said with a little sigh, "what's up?"

I shrugged. "I'm on my way to Spanish." Why did everything seem so strange since we'd gotten home? Talking to Dana had never been tough like this before. "Where are you going?" I tried.

She held up a textbook. "Math."

"Oh," I said. I wasn't sure what to say. "Listen, Dana," I said at last. "Maybe we can get together. You know, later."

"You mean like after school?" she said.

"Yeah, sure," I said. Then I remembered—my dad was supposed to pick me up and take me to Mack's right after school. "Actually, I just remembered, I can't today," I told her. "What about tomorrow?"

"No, tomorrow I can't," Dana said. "Tomorrow's my first Drama Club rehearsal." She paused and looked at me. "I got in, by the way."

"In?" I repeated, confused.

"Drama Club," she said. "I got into the play."

"Oh, that's great," I said, still thinking. "Listen, Thursday's out for me because it's the first practice for the J.V. team."

"Oh. Okay," said Dana.

Neither one of us said anything. The bell rang.

"I guess we're going to be late for class," Dana pointed out, shifting her weight a little.

"Yeah, I guess so," I said. I turned to go.

"Michael," Dana said suddenly.

"Yeah?" I said, turning back toward her.

"Well, I was just thinking," she said in a low voice. "I know we're both busy, but maybe we can still get together, sort of. I mean, it doesn't have to be anything special, right? You know, maybe you could just stop by the theater during my rehearsal tomorrow, or I could come watch you practice on Thursday or something."

"Oh, no, I don't think you'd better come to practice," I answered quickly. I was pretty sure it wouldn't look good to Coach Newman if Dana showed up with me for the first practice, especially since I hadn't made the team yet—or the first cut, even. "I really have to show the coach that I'm serious, you know?"

"Yeah, sure. No problem," Dana said shortly, almost cutting me off.

"But I guess maybe I could come by your rehearsal," I said, a little hesitantly. Like I said, I always got the feeling those Drama Club people were kind of snobby. I really wasn't excited by the thought of walking into an auditorium full of them. Besides, Dana's two friends would be there, and I definitely had the feeling they weren't too crazy about me.

"I should probably work out at the gym tomorrow after school, though," I went on. "You know, maybe swim a few laps in the pool or something."

"Okay, fine, Michael," said Dana. Her voice sounded funny, a little tight. "I've got to go. I'm going to be late." She turned to go.

I watched her take a few steps. I felt like I should say something.

"Maybe I could stop by the theater later, you know, toward the end," I called after her finally.

She didn't turn around.

"Whatever," she said again, her voice still sounding funny.

I stood there and watched her head down the hall, her long, flowered skirt swinging a little. She walked to the end of the hall and turned the corner. She didn't look back at me once.

The next morning I jogged down the same hall on my way to English class, the one class Dana and I had together. I glanced at my watch. I had about thirty seconds until the final bell, and I managed to slip into the classroom just as it rang. Mr. Matthews raised his eyebrows as I quickly slid into the empty seat beside Dana.

I turned to look at her and saw that she was staring at me, her eyes wide and her mouth slightly open.

"Michael, what did you *do*?" she whispered. She put her hand up to her head, and I suddenly realized what she was talking about—my haircut.

I grinned and shrugged a little. "It's for the team," I whispered back.

Mr. Matthews cleared his throat. "Okay, everyone, let's talk about the chapters you read for today. Who would like to tell me what's going on with our main characters?"

Nicole Yardley, who was sitting a couple of seats to my right, raised her hand and started to speak. I opened my notebook and glanced back at Dana. She was still staring at me.

"They made you do that for the *football team*?" she whispered, her eyes still wide.

"Not exactly," I said under my breath. Why was she making such a big deal out of this? "It's just a haircut," I whispered.

"Excuse me," said Mr. Matthews sharply. "Michael Tyler and Dana Bryant, if you two can't stop talking during class, I'm going to have to ask one of you to find a new seat."

"Sorry, Mr. Matthews," I answered. I bent over my notebook and sneaked a glance at Dana, but she was studying her own notebook intently. Her head was turned slightly away from me, and I couldn't see her face.

Later that day, after school, as I was making my way down the steps of the gym to the lower level, where the pool is, I ran into Bruce on his way up. He was wearing red swim trunks, and he had a towel around his neck.

He grinned when he saw me. "Hey, Tyler. How's it going?"

"Pretty good, I guess," I answered.

He cocked his head. "You sure? You look like you've got something on your mind."

The truth was, I'd been thinking about Dana

again. She hadn't said much to me when English class ended, and I hadn't run into her for the rest of the day. I had a weird feeling about her. She definitely seemed upset about something. Like that stuff today in English about the haircut—like it was some big heavy thing that I'd gone to the barber. As if my haircut had anything to do with *her*.

"Nah, I'm okay. Just thinking about working out with the team tomorrow," I lied.

"You'd better be," said Bruce. He gave me a quick punch in the stomach and laughed. "It's going to be tough out there. Hey, nice clip."

"Huh? Oh, you mean the hair," I said, raising my hand to my head.

"Definitely a good move," said Bruce. "Doesn't give the guys on the other side anything to hang on to, you know?" He grinned. "Not to mention the girls really go for it."

"Yeah, well, whatever," I said, thinking of Dana. "Listen, I'm going to swim a few laps. Catch you later."

"Okay, see you, Tyler," he said, waving as I headed down the stairs.

One thing about having short hair, even if Dana didn't like it, it was great for swimming. I didn't have to wear a cap, and I felt totally streamlined, like I was moving through the water more quickly than ever before.

Forty-five minutes later, I was finished with my swim and had showered and dressed. I glanced at my watch and wondered if Dana's rehearsal was still going on. I figured if I dropped by toward the end, there might not be as many Drama Club people hanging around. And if Dana was through, maybe we could get together.

And do what? I couldn't help wondering. It wasn't like we were at the lake, where we could go for a bike ride in the woods or even just take a walk in the sand. I supposed we could go get something to eat somewhere. But where? Bruce had mentioned a place called Stevie's, near school, where the guys from the team hung out with their girlfriends sometimes. But I didn't really want to take Dana there. The place would probably be full of football players and cheerleaders. If we showed up there, Bruce and the other guys were bound to start asking me a whole bunch of questions about Dana. And hadn't I decided it would be better to keep Dana and football separate?

Finally, I decided to just head over to the theater and find out what Dana felt like doing. The only problem was, I wasn't quite sure where the theater was. I knew I'd seen some kind of sign for it back in the main school building, though, so I headed back that way, around the soccer field.

Inside the main building, the halls were pretty much empty, since school was out for the day. I wandered around for a few minutes and finally spotted a custodian in a green uniform sweeping the floor at the end of a hall on the second floor.

"Excuse me," I asked the man. "Can you tell me how to get to the theater?"

"You want the main entrance, or you want to go in on the upper level?" he asked.

I shrugged. "Doesn't matter. Whatever's closer."

"That'd be up here," he answered. "You just go through the double doors down that way, make a left, then make your second right, and then a left again. Open the red door marked 'B'."

"Okay, thanks," I said, memorizing the directions.

I headed down the halls, and soon I arrived at the door marked "B." Pulling it open, I realized that it led to the theater's balcony. The rows of red velvet seats were dark, but I could see three people standing on the illuminated stage below. Dana wasn't one of them, but I recognized her friend with the dark hair. Carla, I thought she'd said her name was. I wondered if Dana had left.

Then, suddenly, I heard voices. As my eyes adjusted to the light, I saw that there were two people sitting in the front row of balcony seats, their backs to me. They were talking, and I recognized one of the voices as Dana's. I started to make my way up to where she was sitting.

"I've made a decision," Dana said.

"Oh?" said another girl, whose voice I thought I recognized as the other one of Dana's friends I'd met, the one with the long, curly hair. "What's that?"

"I've decided I can't do it," said Dana. "I can't let myself be tied down to one person right now."

I stopped in my tracks. Was she talking about *me*?

"But he's a wonderful boy," said her friend. "You don't find boys like that so easily, you know."

I had to admit, if they were talking about me I was kind of surprised. I hadn't thought that Dana's friends liked me much. I took a few steps back into the shadows to listen some more.

"I know, I know," Dana replied. "And that's what makes this so difficult, don't you see? But I'm just not ready for a wonderful boy right now, not when there's so much else I want to do and see."

I felt myself getting angry. What was she talking about? Was she planning on breaking up with me? I listened some more.

"What are you going to tell him?" asked Dana's friend.

Dana paused. "The truth. It's the only way. I know it will hurt him, but I hope someday he'll understand."

She *was* talking about me! Suddenly, I felt kind of sick. I couldn't listen to this anymore. I stumbled back through the darkness to the door and pushed my way back out into the hall.

So that was what was wrong with Dana—she'd decided she didn't want to go out with me anymore. Well, I could take that. I didn't like it, but I could take it. But if that was what she really wanted, why didn't she just come out and tell me? I pounded my fist angrily into my hand. Why couldn't Dana be honest with me? Why did she have to play all these silly games?

Chapter 7

Dana

"What are you going to tell him?" Sophie read.

I scanned my lines briefly, then tried to say them by heart. "The truth. It's the only way. I know it will hurt him, but I hope someday he'll understand."

Sophie paused. "Maybe it will help you to know that *I* understand, Amanda," she said.

"Thank you, Mother," I finished.

Sophie closed her script. "That was great, Dana."

"Did I do okay?" I asked hopefully. "I tried to do as much as I could without looking at the script."

"It was great," Sophie reassured me. "You were totally convincing. I practically felt like I was about to cry or something, listening to you."

"Thanks, Soph," I said, giving her a quick hug. "And thanks for going over my lines with me."

"No problem," she said. She sighed. "I wish I really *was* playing the mother, though. I can't believe I'm only the neighbor. It's such a small part. Even Carla got a bigger role than I did, and she doesn't even want to be an actress.''

I looked at Sophie sympathetically. It was strange how things had worked out. Carla wasn't nearly as into acting as Sophie, but Carla had ended up playing Lydia, the sister of Jonathan, the guy Amanda's parents want her to marry. It wasn't a huge role, nowhere near as big as Amanda, but Carla definitely had a lot more lines than Sophie, who was only in two scenes.

Of course, I was incredibly happy to be playing Amanda. It was a big role, the lead, which meant memorizing a lot of lines. Sophie and Carla had both promised to help me, though. That's what I loved about my friends. They were there for me when I was feeling down, and when something good happened to me, they never acted jealous or anything. They were really happy for me.

Unlike Michael, I thought with a pang. When I'd seen him yesterday morning, he hadn't even *asked* me how the auditions went. And when I told him I'd gotten into the play, he didn't seem to care. He was too busy talking about all that football stuff of his.

It definitely seemed like now that we were back in Greenfield, football was more important to Michael than I was. Football was the reason he never had any time to get together with me, and football was practically all he talked about when I saw him in school. Football was even the reason he'd gotten that awful haircut!

It had really hurt my feelings that Michael had gone and cut off all his hair without even mentioning anything to me about it. I mean, not that he had to ask me for *permission* or anything, but I knew I'd never go and totally change my whole appearance without finding out what he thought about the idea first.

But maybe that was my big mistake. Maybe I cared about Michael *too* much, more than he cared about me. He *had* been acting very different around me, and we hadn't seen each other once outside school since we got back from the lake. And he had forgotten to call me the other night even though *he* was the one who'd said we should talk.

Then there was the way he'd reacted when I'd said that maybe I could come watch his football practice. He'd obviously hated the idea. Not that I really wanted to watch the football team run around on the field, but I thought guys were supposed to like that stuff, when their girlfriends showed up to watch them practice.

And now that the Drama Club rehearsal was almost over, it seemed pretty obvious that he wasn't going to show up *here*, either. I could have kicked myself for even suggesting it to him. The more I thought about it, the more obvious the whole thing was—Michael just wasn't that interested in me anymore.

*   *   *

"Ooooh, look at this one!" said Sophie excitedly. She picked up a purple beret with a cluster of pink and white flowers, plopped it on her head, and struck a pose. "What do you guys think?"

Carla looked up from the earrings she was examining. "That looks great on you, Sophie. Don't you think so, Dana?"

"Yeah, it's nice," I answered halfheartedly.

It was Friday, and Sophie and Carla and I were shopping at the mall after school. Usually I loved checking out the stores with my friends, but today my heart just wasn't in it. Michael had never shown up at rehearsal on Wednesday afternoon, and we'd barely said anything to each other since then. Now it was the beginning of the weekend, and Michael and I didn't have any plans to see each other. I couldn't believe this was happening.

"Hey, Dana, this one would be really cute on you, with your hair," said Sophie. She handed me a red hat with an upturned brim. "Here, try it on."

I shook my head. "No, thanks," I said. "That's okay."

Sophie and Carla exchanged glances.

"Dana," said Carla in a serious voice, "what's going on?"

I paused. I supposed I should probably tell them about Michael. After all, they were my best friends. Besides, maybe they'd have an idea of what I should do. But I knew if I started talking about it, I'd probably burst out into tears right here in the mall.

Sophie looked concerned. "Dana, you seem so down. What is it? Is something wrong between you and Michael?"

I nodded, feeling the tears spring to my eyes. I blinked them back.

"Oh, Dana," said Carla, putting a hand on my arm. "Did he break up with you?"

"Not yet," I said, choking back a little sob. "You guys, it's all so . . . *terrible*. I don't know what to do."

"Why? What's going on?" asked Sophie.

I wiped away a tear.

"Come on," said Carla quickly. "let's sit over here, where no one will see us." She pulled me over to a bench behind some potted trees.

We all sat down.

"Now, tell us everything," Carla commanded.

"Carla's right," said Sophie. "You'll feel better if you talk about it, Dana."

But I doubted that anything could make me feel better right now.

"I'm not sure exactly *what's* going on," I told them. "All I know is that Michael is acting totally different toward me." I took a deep breath. "It started as soon as we got back to Greenfield, the first day of school. He seemed sort of . . . I don't know . . . like he wasn't that excited to see me or something. And it's just been getting worse since then.

When I saw him today in school, he hardly said anything at all to me.''

"What about when you're alone?" asked Sophie. "What's he like then?"

"We haven't ever *been* alone since we got back," I complained. "We haven't even talked on the phone. There was one night we were supposed to, but he never called and I just couldn't get up the nerve to call *him*."

"I'd say *he's* the one with nerve if he didn't call you when he was supposed to," commented Carla angrily.

"Really," agreed Sophie. "What kind of boyfriend is it who never calls you or sees you outside of school?"

"That's what I've been wondering," I admitted. "Michael hasn't even asked me about this weekend. I don't even know if we're supposed to get together." I sighed. "Oh, you guys, I bet he wants to break up with me."

"Not necessarily," said Carla. "I mean, if he wanted to break up with you, he would just do it, wouldn't he? Still, you can't let him treat you like this, Dana."

I sniffed. "But what am I supposed to do?"

"Well, first of all, you can't just keep waiting around for him," said Carla firmly.

"It's true," said Sophie. "You're leaving everything up to *him*, like anytime he wants to see you, he can."

"Take this weekend, for instance," said Carla. "If Michael wanted to see you sometime this weekend, he should have said something about it already. He can't leave everything until the last minute and expect you to be free."

"But I *am* free," I pointed out. "Besides, Michael and I aren't used to making plans in advance like that. At the lake—"

"But this isn't the lake," Carla cut me off. "You're back in Greenfield now, and things are different. You have other things to do besides hang around waiting for Michael to call, and Michael's just going to have to realize that." She smiled. "Besides, you're *not* free this weekend."

I looked at her, confused. "I'm not?"

Carla smiled at Sophie, and Sophie shook her head at me.

"Oh, no," said Sophie. "You're incredibly busy. Isn't she, Carla?"

"As a matter of fact, I don't think she has a single free moment," said Carla. "After all, there's shopping now, and then we're going for pizza together—"

"Right," Sophie went on, "and later we're all supposed to go over to my house and watch TV and make hot fudge sundaes."

I smiled in spite of myself. Carla and Sophie could be so funny sometimes.

"And then there's that marathon study session for the history test we plan to have at my house tomorrow," added Carla.

"And after that, of course, we're going to reward ourselves by going to the movies," put in Sophie.

I laughed, wiping away the last of my tears.

"You guys are great," I said. They each put an arm around me, and I pulled them to me for a quick hug. "You're the best friends in the whole world."

"That's what friends are for," said Carla. "Anyway, it'll be lots of fun, you'll see."

"That's right, Dana," said Sophie. "We're going to have such a good time this weekend, you're going to forget all about Michael."

I managed a smile. I only hoped it was true.

CHAPTER 8

Michael

"Okay, boys, that's it for today!" called Coach Newman. "The cut list will be posted outside my office on Monday."

I leaned my hands on my knees and took a few deep breaths. My second practice with the team had been a tough one. The coach had had us doing wind sprints, running from the end zone to the ten-yard line, back to the end zone and on to the twenty-yard line, back again and to the thirty-yard line, and so on, for the entire length of the field. It was definitely an exhausting way to spend a Saturday morning.

But I knew I was going to have to be able to take it if I wanted to make the next cut. Four guys had already been cut after the first practice, and three of them were freshmen, like me. It was going to take everything I had to prove to the coach that I was ready to be a Hornet.

Bruce jogged over to me and gave me a quick slap on the back.

"Tyler, you looked alright out there today," he said.

"Thanks," I said, wiping the sweat from my forehead. "I just hope Coach thinks so, too."

"Don't worry, you'll make the cut," Bruce assured me.

I wished I could be as confident about it as he was, but I knew I hadn't performed my best that day. The trouble was, I just kept thinking about Dana. After the way she'd been acting, and especially after what I'd overheard on the balcony on Wednesday, I was sure she'd been about to break it off with me. But I'd seen her in school a couple of times since then, and she had hardly said anything at all.

"Hey, Tyler, we're all going over to Stevie's tonight to grab some burgers and stuff," said Bruce. "You should come."

I shrugged. "I don't know, Bruce." Even though Dana had been pretty cold to me these past couple of days, I couldn't help wondering what she was up to tonight. I knew that if we were still at the lake, we definitely would have spent the evening together.

"Come on," Bruce said again. "Lots of the varsity guys are going to be there, too."

"Well, maybe," I said.

"I'll call you later," Bruce offered. "I've got my dad's car this weekend, so I can pick you up if you want to go." He gave me another slap on the back. "Catch you later, Tyler."

"Okay, see you," I called after him.

As I made my way toward the locker room, I found myself thinking about Dana again. The way she was acting was really getting on my nerves. I mean, if she wanted to break up with me, why didn't she just do it and get it over with? If there was one thing I really hated, it was stupid games.

That's when I made up my mind. I was going over to Dana's house right now to ask her what was going on. The way I saw it, if Dana was trying to get the message across to me by the way she'd been acting, she might as well just come out and say it to my face.

The address on the class list was "2326 Maple Avenue." And as I made my way down Elm toward Maple, I couldn't help thinking how strange it was that I'd never even seen Dana's house in Greenfield. I knew she'd probably be pretty surprised that I was just showing up like this, but I didn't care. I wanted to know the truth, to get some answers once and for all.

I rounded the corner onto Maple and spotted a group of little kids tossing a softball around in the street. As I got closer, I realized that one of them was Arnie, Dana's little brother, so I waved to him.

He gave me a blank stare.

"Arnie, hi," I said. "Remember me?"

"Oh, yeah," he said, his face finally lighting up with recognition.

I shook my head in amazement. Dana's little brother always seemed to have his head somewhere in the clouds. I remembered that Dana had said he had my old teacher, Mrs. Fletcher, for fifth grade this year. Mrs. Fletcher was tough, and I bet she was giving Arnie a pretty hard time.

"I'm looking for Dana," I told him. "Which one is your house?"

He pointed at a white house with green shutters just down the street. "Over there."

"Okay, thanks," I said, heading off in that direction.

A moment or two later, he called after me. "Dana's not there, though!"

I stopped and turned back toward him. "Where is she?"

He shrugged. "She went out someplace with her friends. My mom and Jeff are out, too." He grinned. "But they said I could stay and play 'cause Brian Hansen's mom said she would watch me out her window."

"Come on, Arn!" called one of the other kids. "Let's play!"

"Listen, Arnie," I said quickly. "When Dana comes back, tell her that I was here looking for her, okay? Tell her to call me."

"Okay," said Arnie, already taking off down the street after the other kids.

*   *   *

At seven o'clock that evening, the phone finally rang. I picked it up.

It was Bruce. "Hey, Tyler, that you?"

"Yeah, it's me," I answered. "Hi, Bruce, how're you doing?"

"Great," he answered. "Listen, I'm about to leave for Stevie's, and I thought I'd swing by and pick you up."

I thought a moment. I certainly didn't feel like sitting around all night waiting for Dana to come home. I guessed I might as well go to Stevie's with Bruce and the other guys. Maybe it would take my mind off Dana.

"Okay, sure," I told him.

"See you in fifteen minutes," said Bruce. He paused. "Oh, and Tyler, I've got the feeling you're going to be *really* happy you decided to come."

"Huh?" I said. What was Bruce talking about? But before I had a chance to ask him what he meant, he hung up.

A few minutes later, I heard the toot of a car horn outside. I grabbed my jacket, said good-bye to my mom in the living room, and hurried out the front door. Bruce had pulled up in front of the house in a red sports car and was waiting for me.

"Hi," I said as I climbed into the passenger seat.

"Nice car, huh? My dad lets me use it on week-ends sometimes," said Bruce. He gunned the motor and pulled the car out into the street with a lurch.

"The girls really go for it, if you know what I mean."

I didn't say anything. I couldn't help thinking of Dana. Somehow, I couldn't imagine her caring that much about a car.

As Bruce meandered through the streets of Greenfield, I suddenly realized that he wasn't headed toward the high school.

"I thought you said Stevie's was near school," I said, a little confused.

"It is," he said. "But we have to stop to pick up the girls first."

"Girls?" I repeated.

"Well, sure," said Bruce. "Ashley, my girlfriend. She lives just up here, on Oak Street." He grinned at me. "And she's got her friend Cindy with her, too."

"Oh," I said. "Okay." When Bruce had talked about the guys going over to Stevie's tonight, I hadn't realized that there would be girls going, too. But I supposed it made sense. It was Saturday night, after all. Bruce probably wanted to see his girlfriend.

"Cindy's real cute," said Bruce. He grinned at me again. "Blonde, with blue eyes. I think you're going to like her."

I stared at him. What was Bruce saying? Was he trying to fix me up with Cindy?

"Oh, no, that's okay," I began. "You see—"

"Relax, Tyler," Bruce cut me off. "No strings attached. I only told Ashley to bring her along, just in case. If you like her, fine. If you're not interested, no big deal. She's definitely a cute one, though. In fact, I almost went out with her instead of Ashley.''

"Oh," I said, thinking. I supposed maybe I should have told Bruce about Dana to begin with. I wondered if I should tell him now. But that didn't seem like such a great idea, not now that she was probably going to break up with me. I guessed it was no big deal that this Cindy girl was coming. After all, Bruce had said there were no strings attached, so it wasn't like a *date* or anything. She was just coming because she was Ashley's friend, right?

A few moments later, we pulled up in front of a sprawling, one-story gray house. Bruce beeped his horn. A minute later, the front door opened, and two girls came running out. One of them had long, curly, red hair, and the other one had a short blond ponytail tied with a red ribbon.

The redhead leaned into the driver's-side window and planted a kiss on Bruce's cheek.

"Hi, Ash," said Bruce. He turned to me. "Get in the back, will you, Tyler?"

"Oh, uh, sure," I said.

I pushed open my door and climbed out. The blond girl, who was still standing by the car, smiled at me a little shyly. Bruce was right, she *was* pretty.

"Hi," she said. "I'm Cindy. You're Michael, right?"

"Um, right," I answered. "Nice to meet you," I added.

I flipped the front seat forward and Cindy climbed in and slid across the back to make room for me. I got in beside her.

Ashley settled herself in the front, next to Bruce, and we took off. The back seat was pretty cramped, and Cindy and I were sort of squished together. I could feel the sleeve of her fuzzy white sweater against the skin of my arm. She flashed me a smile. I smiled back, a little awkwardly.

"Bruce says you're going out for the J.V. team," Cindy said.

"Yeah, Tyler's going to make it, too," said Bruce from the front seat.

"I hope so," I said, pleased with what Bruce had said.

"Me, too," said Cindy shyly. "That would mean I'd be cheering you at the games."

"Cindy's a J.V. cheerleader, like me," Ashley explained. "We've got a really great squad this year, and we're working on some amazing routines."

"Those girls are awesome. They definitely get some of the credit for the Hornets' winning record," commented Bruce. He put an arm around Ashley and pulled her closer to him.

Cindy gazed at me, and I turned to look out the window. This was starting to seem an awful lot like a double date, and it was making me kind of uncomfortable.

A moment later, we pulled into the parking lot in front of Stevie's. The lot was filled with cars, and there was a crowd of kids visible through the plate-glass windows. I could hear music coming from inside. Bruce and Ashley climbed out, and I hurried to get out of the car, too.

Cindy was right by my side. "Wow, it looks like *everybody's* here tonight," she said excitedly.

"Yeah," I said, feeling a little guilty. I felt kind of bad for Cindy. It definitely seemed like she had the idea that we were supposed to be here *together*. I wasn't sure what to do.

We followed Bruce and Ashley inside. There were tons of kids in there, standing around in groups, leaning up against the counter, and overflowing from the booths by the window.

"Come on, let's get a seat!" called Bruce above the music.

I looked around doubtfully. "I don't think there are any left."

"Don't worry about it," he said, flashing me a grin. "There's always room at *our* tables. Come on, follow me."

We made our way through the crowd to a couple of tables in the corner, where I saw Cal Harrison, Mark Rapetti, Greg Stone, and a bunch of other guys I recognized sitting with some girls.

"Hey, Tyler, how's it going?" Greg greeted me. "You making the J.V. cuts okay?"

"So far," I said.

Greg slid over a bit to make room for me on the bench where he was sitting. He put his arm around a blond girl next to him. "This is Kirsten."

"Hi," I said, taking a seat.

She smiled. "Nice to meet you. Your name's Tyler?"

"Michael Tyler, actually," I told her.

"Tyler's going out for J.V.," said Greg. "He's a freshman. His big brother's Matt Tyler."

"I remember Matt," said Kirsten. "He was nice."

Greg turned to me. "Coach Newman's pretty tough, but he's a good coach. If you can hang in there and keep making the cuts, he'll make you into the best player you can be."

"That's what I hear," I said.

Kirsten smiled at me. "Did you come here by yourself?"

"Kind of," I answered. "I mean, Bruce Eakin drove me over."

I glanced at Cindy, who was standing a little way away, talking intently with Ashley. Cindy was definitely pretty, there was no doubt about that. And she seemed nice, too. I began to think about Dana again, about all the fun we'd had at the lake together—riding our bikes, watching the sun set by the lake, and just being together. Then I thought about how badly things had gone between us ever since we'd gotten back to Greenfield. How different she'd acted, and how I'd overheard her talking about wanting to break up with me.

Then, for the first time, I began to wonder, could it be that Dana was right to want to end things? Could it be that what we had at the lake was just a summer romance and nothing more?

Chapter 9

Dana

"Wasn't that unbelievable?" sighed Sophie as we stepped out of the movie theater and into the cool night air.

"Unbelievable is right," scoffed Carla. "Two people who *happen* to survive the same plane crash, and then *happen* to meet again on another plane that crashes a year later, and not only do they both survive again, but they fall in love, too?" She shook her head. "Nobody would believe that story."

"Well, I liked it," said Sophie, twirling in her vintage scarf-dress, which she was wearing again. "I thought it was romantic, especially the end, when they decide to get married while skydiving."

"That part was pretty good," I agreed.

Going to the movies with Carla and Sophie had been fun. And it had helped take my mind off Michael for a little while. Still, as the three of us walked down the street together, I couldn't help wondering what he was doing now, and if he had called my house.

"Maybe I should call home," I said, spotting a phone booth.

"Why?" asked Sophie. "Your mom knows you're sleeping at my house tonight, right?"

I nodded. "But maybe I should just kind of . . . check in."

"You mean check in to see if Michael called, don't you?" said Carla.

"Well, yeah," I admitted.

"Dana," Carla said sternly, "you called home right before we went to the movies, and your mom said no one had called for you. You can't keep waiting and hoping like this for Michael to call."

"Really," agreed Sophie. "You should try to put Michael out of your mind for now. Let's all just have a fun night together, like we said."

"Sophie's right," said Carla.

"Okay, okay, I won't call," I said. I still couldn't believe it, though. Here it was, Saturday night, and I hadn't heard anything at all from Michael since I'd seen him in school on Friday. We'd never gone a whole day before without seeing each other or talking.

Carla checked her watch. "Okay, it's still pretty early. Where should we go now? You want to hit the mall again? There are probably some places still open."

"I have an idea," said Sophie. "Let's go to Stevie's."

"Is that that place near school?" asked Carla.

Sophie nodded. "This girl in my French class, Kelly, said lots of the kids from Hyde go there on the weekends."

"Okay, great," said Carla. She turned to me. "Is that alright with you, Dana?"

I shrugged. I didn't really feel much like going anywhere. But I knew my friends were only trying to help me feel better.

"Okay, I'll go," I said.

Sophie linked her arm through mine.

"Who knows, Dana," she said, giving me a squeeze. "This could end up being your lucky night. Maybe you'll run into some really cute guy from school there."

"Wow, this looks great!" Sophie said excitedly as we climbed the two cement steps leading to the entrance to Stevie's. "I bet everybody from Hyde is here tonight!"

"Sophie," said Carla, pushing open the glass door, "there isn't room in this place for everybody from Hyde. One *tenth* of the kids from Hyde couldn't fit in here."

"Whatever," said Sophie, waving her hand around in the air. "It looks like fun."

The place certainly was crowded—and noisy. There were kids everywhere, and loud music was playing on the jukebox in the corner. We pushed our way through the crowd.

"I don't think there are any seats," said Carla, looking around. "We might have to stand until someone leaves."

"I have to use the bathroom," I said. "I'll be right back."

"Okay, we'll keep an eye out for a table," said Sophie.

I could see a sign that said "REST ROOMS" high up on the far wall, and I headed in that direction. Soon I had broken through the thickest part of the crowd. I passed by a couple of crowded tables and opened the door to the women's room. Amazingly, there was an empty stall, so I took it.

A moment later, I heard two girls come in and stop in front of the sinks.

"Okay, what do you think, Ashley?" said one of them. "Is my hair okay like this?"

"It looks really cute," answered the other one. "And I *love* that new sweater, Cindy."

"Thanks," said Cindy. "I got it at that new store at the mall, the one called Cookie's."

"Well, it looks great on you," said Ashley.

"I just hope Michael thinks so," said Cindy.

Michael? I was reaching to unlock the door of the stall, but I paused. That's silly, I told myself. Michael's a really common name; there must be a hundred of them at Hyde High. She must be talking about someone else.

"I know, he's really cute," said Ashley. "Bruce says he's probably going to make the J.V. team, too."

I froze. J.V. team? Was she talking about football? There might be a hundred Michaels at Hyde High, but how many of them could be trying to make the football team? Then I thought of something—*Bruce,* hadn't that been what Michael had called that big guy with the short hair the first day at school? I waited to see what they would say next.

"I just can't tell if he's really interested or not," said Cindy. "I mean, he's been talking to Greg Stone since we got here."

"You know how guys are," said Ashley. "They're probably totally involved in some football conversation."

I swallowed. So it *was* the football team they were talking about. I peeked through the crack of the stall door. Two girls, one with long, red hair and one with a short blond ponytail tied with a red ribbon were standing in front of the mirror.

"Yeah, I guess you're right," said Cindy, the blond one. "He *was* kind of leaning against me in the back seat on the way over here, you know, like he wanted to get close."

"Well, that's a good sign," said Ashley. "Anyway, Bruce said he thought Michael would probably like you. That's why we decided to fix you guys up tonight."

I stared at them in astonishment. That had *better*

not be my Michael they were talking about. It couldn't be, could it? I mean, sure, things had been pretty strange between Michael and me lately, but he would never do something like that, would he?

"Listen," Ashley went on, "let's go back out there. I'll try and get Kirsten into a conversation so there's some room on that bench. Then maybe you can ask Greg to slide down a little to make room for you next to Michael."

"Okay, sounds good," said Cindy.

"I'm sure all you need to do is to manage to sit next to him and talk to him a little," said Ashley, as they headed for the door. "You know, kind of get to know him better."

"I'll talk to him about football," said Cindy, pulling open the door. "They *always* want to talk about that."

When they'd left the rest room, I stepped out of the stall. I had a really sick feeling in my stomach. I knew it was silly. There was no way that the Michael they were talking about could have been Michael Tyler, *my* Michael, right? It must have been about some other Michael trying out for the football team, I told myself.

Just then the door opened and three girls came in laughing and chattering. I quickly splashed some cold water on my face. As I did it, I noticed that my hands were trembling.

I pushed through the crowd in the bathroom to the door. Suddenly, I wanted to go home. I didn't want to spend the evening at Stevie's with all these people, and I didn't want to go back to Sophie's to sleep over. I knew my friends had just been trying to keep me busy so I wouldn't have time to be upset about Michael, and I appreciated it, but I really didn't feel like doing anything right now. I just wanted to go home to my own bed and curl up and fall asleep. I decided to go and find Carla and Sophie and tell them I wanted to leave.

I stepped out into the noisy, crowded room. I threaded my way through a group of people hanging around the jukebox, and edged past the two crowded tables in the corner.

As I did, something caught my eye—a blond ponytail with a red ribbon. It was Cindy, the girl from the bathroom. She was sitting at one of the tables, talking enthusiastically, her ponytail bobbing up and down. On one side of her was a stocky blond guy I thought I recognized from school.

And on the other side of her was Michael!

Chapter 10

Michael

"Dana!" I couldn't believe my eyes. There she was, standing right in front of me. I stood up, leaving Cindy in mid-sentence, and walked toward her. "What are you doing here?"

Dana stared at me, her jaw clenched.

"Don't even talk to me, Michael," she said.

"What?" I said, feeling myself start to get angry. I lowered my voice. "What is your problem?"

"*My* problem?" she said, her eyes widening. "How can you even say that, when here you are—" She broke off, biting her lip, and looked away.

Just then, Dana's two friends walked over.

"Oh, wow," said the reddish-haired one, Sophie. "Michael, hi. We didn't know you were here."

"We sure didn't," muttered Carla, the other one.

"Yeah, well, obviously Michael didn't know *we* were going to be here, either," Dana spat out.

I stared at them. Was Dana actually *angry* with me for going to Stevie's? It wasn't like we'd made plans for tonight or anything. And what about all that stuff I'd heard her saying to Sophie the other day? Wasn't she the one who'd said she didn't want to be "tied down" anymore?

"Dana, hang on a minute," I said.

"Forget it, Michael," said Dana. She turned to her friends. "Come on, you guys, let's go." She glared for a moment in the direction of the bench where I'd been sitting. "Have *fun*, Michael."

They left, and I turned slowly around to face the table. Greg and Cindy and Bruce and Ashley were all looking at me. Cindy stood up.

"Is everything okay, Michael?" she asked.

"Yeah, fine," I answered numbly.

Then I realized Dana was probably angry because she'd seen me with Cindy. But that was ridiculous. I wasn't really *with* Cindy. I mean, sure, she was sitting next to me, but she was sitting next to Greg, too. For all Dana knew, Cindy was Greg's girlfriend, right?

Bruce stood up and ushered me back to the table.

"Come on back and join the party, Tyler," he said heartily.

Slowly, I sat back down, still thinking about what had just happened. Why had Dana been so nasty? Was it just because I'd been sitting *next* to another girl? That didn't make any sense. But then again, nothing made much sense lately when it came to Dana.

"Who was that girl?" asked Ashley, leaning toward me. "Does she go to our school? Do you know her?"

"Her name's Dana," I answered quietly.

"Boy, that red-haired one she was with had on some getup, huh?" cracked Bruce. "Looked like she was wearing a bunch of rags, don't you think?"

"Actually, to me it looked like she was wearing a *dress*," I snapped. Suddenly I was tired of Bruce, tired of Stevie's and the whole crowd. I stood up.

"Whoa, excuse *me*," said Bruce sarcastically. "I didn't realize they were *friends* of yours, Tyler."

"Well, they are," I said, irritated. "Or one of them is. At least, she used to be . . ." I sighed. "Look, you guys, don't listen to me. I'm just in a bad mood or something. I guess I'd better go."

"Sorry, bud, but I'm not ready to leave yet," said Bruce.

"That's okay," I told him. "I'll walk. It's not far."

"Michael, are you really sure you want to walk?" asked Cindy, looking concerned. "I mean, we could probably find you a ride."

"That's okay. It's a nice night out," I told her. "Besides, I could use some fresh air."

She looked at me, and for a moment, I thought she was going to offer to walk with me. But she just smiled.

"Okay," she said finally. "It was nice meeting you, Michael. Good luck. I hope you make the team."

"Thanks." I managed a smile back. Cindy was okay. It wasn't her fault if she thought she was coming to Stevie's as my date. I felt kind of bad for her. "It was nice meeting you, too, Cindy," I said.

Outside, I took a deep breath of the cool evening air. I started walking down Hyde Lane, in the direction of my house. It felt good to be outside, by myself. A lot of stuff had happened in the week that I'd been home from the lake, and I wasn't even sure what most of it meant. All I knew was that everything Dana and I used to have seemed to be gone.

It was hard to believe that just one week ago the two of us had been sitting together eating corn and barbecued chicken by the lake, watching the sun go down. My summer with Dana had been one of the best summers ever. But now I realized that was *all* it was ever going to be for Dana and me—a great summer.

It wasn't until I was practically in front of Dana's house that I realized I'd missed the turn-off onto Birch Street, and headed down Maple instead. It was no big deal, though. I could just keep going down Maple and head back down around Ash to Birch, the long way.

But for some reason, I didn't keep going down Maple. For some reason, I stopped right where I was and stared up at Dana's big white house. There was a single light on behind a shade on the second floor. I wondered if it was hers, and what she was doing, what she was thinking right now.

I crossed the street and sat down on the curb, still looking up at the house. As the light in the second-floor window went out, I asked myself again what had gone wrong.

Chapter 11

Dana

My mother knocked lightly on my door. "Dana? Is everything alright, honey?"

"Yeah, everything's fine," I lied, trying not to let it show in my voice that I'd been crying.

She opened my door a crack, and I turned my head away, pretending I was looking for something on my dresser.

"I thought you were staying at Sophie's tonight," she said.

"I decided I felt like coming home," I told her, still fiddling with the things on my dresser. "I'm kind of tired."

"Are you coming down with something, do you think?" she asked.

"No, no, I feel fine," I answered quickly. On the outside, I added silently. But inside I feel just terrible.

"Okay, then, get a good night's sleep," she said finally.

"Good night, Mom," I answered, trying not to let my voice crack.

She closed the door, and I flopped down on my bed. I hugged my pillow as hard as I could and burst into tears. Everything was so awful, and the worst thing about it was that I still didn't understand *why*. Something had gone really wrong between Michael and me, and I didn't even know what it was.

I squeezed my eyes shut, trying to get the image of him and that girl Cindy out of my mind. I couldn't believe he had done that to me, that he'd actually let someone fix him up with another girl like that. It was so unfair. If he didn't want to see me anymore, why hadn't he just come out and said so? It hurt me so much to think that he'd been sneaking around.

A few minutes later, I sat up and wiped away my tears. I reached for the tissues on my night table and blew my nose hard. I was exhausted.

As quickly as I could, I changed into my nightgown and crawled into bed. It's time to start forgetting about Michael, I told myself as I switched off the light.

But I *couldn't* forget about Michael. As I lay there in the dark, staring up at the ceiling, memories of the two of us together filled my mind. I saw us sitting together on the lifeguard stand, watching out for Mr. Greeley so we wouldn't get in trouble. I remembered how we'd goofed around in the water on our days off, splashing and dunking each other and yelling. And I saw us eating ice cream that day in front of the general store—the first time he'd ever kissed me.

This was terrible. All I wanted was to have Michael back. I missed him, missed the fun we used to have together, the way he used to look into my eyes when we held hands. Why did it have to end?

Frustrated and sad, I sat up in bed. I reached for the shade on my window and raised it so I could see the sky. There were only a few stars, and the moon was nearly full. The front yard was glowing in the moonlight.

And there, sitting across the street on the curb, his chin in his hands, was Michael.

CHAPTER 12

Michael

At first, I didn't believe my eyes. She looked like a ghost, floating across the grass in her pale bathrobe. But then she said my name.

"Michael?"

I stood up. "Dana," I said, still not completely ready to believe it was really her.

"Michael, what are you doing out here?" she asked, coming closer.

"I couldn't go straight home. Not yet, anyway," I told her. I shrugged. "I remembered that this one was your house, so I figured I'd stop here for a moment, just to look at it."

"Remembered?" said Dana. "What do you mean?"

"From earlier today," I explained. "When I stopped by."

Her eyes widened. "You came by here today? When?"

Now it was my turn to stare. "Didn't Arnie tell you?"

She sighed. "Of course not." She shook her head. "He never remembers anything."

I can't believe it," I said. "I should have realized he would probably forget to tell you."

Dana looked at me.

"Why were you coming over?" she asked carefully.

"I wanted to talk to you about something," I answered.

"Oh," she said, looking down at her feet.

I paused. "Dana, I heard what you said to your friend about me that day on the balcony at school."

She looked at me, a confused expression on her face. "What day? What are you talking about?"

"Dana, come on," I said, a little irritated. "You know what I mean. The day of your rehearsal. You and your friend Sophie were up on the balcony, talking about me. You didn't know I was there, but I heard everything you said." I looked away. "I know you want to break up with me."

"What?" said Dana. She sank down beside me on the curb. "Michael, I really have no idea what you're talking about. What do you think you heard me say?"

I swallowed. This was really humiliating. Why was she making me spell it all out for her?

"About how you don't want to be tied down to one person right now," I said. "You said there was a lot of other stuff you wanted to do and see, or something like that."

Dana burst out laughing. "Oh, my gosh!" she said.

I stared at her. Was this her idea of a joke?

"I'm glad you think it's so funny," I said angrily.

She put her hand on my arm. "Oh, no, Michael, that's not it at all. You just misunderstood. I wasn't saying what you thought I was saying."

I looked at her. "Dana, I heard you with my own ears," I said.

She shook her head. "Michael, what you heard were lines from a play. Sophie was helping me go over my lines up there in the balcony. I was *rehearsing*."

I stared at her. "You were?"

She nodded. "Here, does this sound familiar?" She cleared her throat. *"I've decided I can't do it. I can't let myself be tied down to one person right now. . . . But he's a wonderful boy. You don't find boys like that so easily, you know. . . . I know. And that's what makes this so difficult, don't you see? But I'm just not ready for a wonderful boy right now, not when there's so much else I want to do and see."*

I couldn't believe my ears. "That was it," I said. "That was just what you said!" I felt myself grinning. "Those were really just lines from a play? You weren't going to break up with me?"

"Of course not," said Dana. Then she grew serious. "In fact, I was pretty sure that *you* were the one who wanted to break up with *me*."

"What are you talking about?" I said. "Where did you get an idea like that?"

"How about from the fact that you were out on a date with another girl tonight?" she said, her voice growing louder.

"That's not true," I protested. "I wasn't on a date with anyone. Bruce, this guy I know from the football team, just asked me if I felt like going out with a bunch of the guys, that's all."

"Don't even try it, Michael," said Dana. "Don't lie. I know Bruce fixed you up with that girl Cindy tonight. I heard her and her friend talking all about it in the bathroom."

"Oh, wow," I said, shaking my head in disbelief. "Listen, Dana, Cindy may have *thought* she was being fixed up with me, but no one bothered to tell *me* about it. Believe me, if I'd known that was what was supposed to happen, I never would have gone to Stevie's with them in the first place."

"You wouldn't have?" asked Dana doubtfully.

"Of course not!" I responded.

"Then why was Cindy talking about how you were snuggling up against her in the back seat of the car on the way over?" she demanded. "She said she thought you were trying to be near her."

I rubbed my forehead with my hand. This was unbelievable. I turned to her.

"Dana, you've got to believe me," I said. "Bruce was driving his father's sports car, and I got crammed into this tiny back seat with her. I was definitely not trying to get any closer to her."

She gazed up at me, her deep brown eyes wide. "You weren't?"

"No," I said softly, "I wasn't. There's only one person I want to be close to, Dana. You know that."

I saw her eyes fill with tears. "Oh, Michael," she said.

I reached out and took her in my arms. She tilted her face up toward mine. Her skin was glowing in the moonlight. I pulled her toward me and kissed her.

Chapter 13

Dana

"I've made a decision," I said, smoothing down the gray wool skirt I was wearing.

"Oh? What's that?" said Helen Rabbers, the girl who was playing Amanda's mother.

"I've decided I can't do it. I can't let myself be tied down to one person right now," I said.

As I said the line, I smiled a little in spite of myself. I knew this was supposed to be a really serious moment for Amanda's character, but I just couldn't help thinking of Michael and the totally huge mixup we'd had all those weeks ago. I quickly covered my smile with one hand, hoping that no one in the audience had caught it.

Helen walked across the stage toward me.

"But he's a wonderful boy," she said. "You don't find boys like that so easily, you know."

"I know. And that's what makes this so difficult,

don't you see?" I said. "But I'm just not ready for a wonderful boy right now, not when there's so much else I want to do and see."

"What are you going to tell him?" asked Helen.

I took a deep breath. "The truth. It's the only way. I know it will hurt him, but I hope someday he'll understand."

Helen took my hands in hers.

"Maybe it will help you to know that *I* understand, Amanda," she said.

I paused. "Thank you, Mother," I said softly.

There was a moment of silence, and then the curtain came down. The theater practically exploded with applause.

Helen gave my hand a squeeze. "We did it!" she said excitedly. "Our last performance."

"I know," I said happily. I listened to the audience still applauding. "I think they liked it."

The rest of the cast came running onto the stage. Sophie and Carla threw their arms around me in a huge hug.

"You were great, Dana," said Carla.

"Incredible," added Sophie, her eyes shining.

I *felt* great. The play had gone really well.

The curtain rose again, and we all grabbed hands for the curtain call. After the group bow, the actors with the larger roles took separate bows. First came Carla and Jeremy Wright, who'd played the butler in the play. Next came Helen and Scott Richards, who'd been Amanda's father, followed by Alex Gerson, who'd played Roger, the guy Amanda was supposed to marry. Finally, it was my turn.

I stepped to the front of the stage, and the applause grew louder. The stage lights were really bright, and I couldn't see anything past the edge of the stage as I took my bow. But suddenly, I heard a group of guys cheering from somewhere off to the right.

I knew it had to be Michael, Greg, and Mark, and the rest of their football buddies.

And there was a howling sound that I was sure could only be coming from Bruce Eakin.

I stepped back into line with the rest of the cast, and we all took our final bow. The curtain went down for the last time.

Everybody began milling around on the stage, talking excitedly.

"That was so much fun," said Sophie. "Even if I did only have a little part."

"You were very good at it," said Carla.

"Yeah," I agreed. "I bet Ms. Gruss gives you a much bigger role in the next play."

"Thanks," said Sophie. "You were both great, too." She hopped up and down. "And now we get to go to the party!"

Carla screwed up her face. "This is going to be really weird, don't you think? You know, because it's a *combination* party and everything."

"I think it sounds fun," said Sophie.

"But half the people there won't even *know* the other half," Carla pointed out.

"That's why it sounds fun," said Sophie, shrugging. "Besides, if it was Dana's idea, I'm sure it will work out."

"I hope so," I said. "It just seemed like the right way to do it. You know, since our last performance happened to be on the same day as the Hornets' opening game and everything."

"And," teased Sophie, "since the star of the play happens to be going out with the J.V. Hornets' full-block."

"That's full*back*," I corrected her, laughing.

"Whatever," said Sophie, waving her hand in the air.

"Really," laughed Carla. "We can't all be football experts like you, Dana."

Half an hour later I made my way through the crowd at Stevie's, looking for Michael.

Suddenly I felt someone throw an arm around my shoulders. It was Bruce.

"Dana, you were *awesome*," he roared.

"Thanks, Bruce," I answered.

He grinned. "Did you hear me yelling there, at the end?"

"Oh, yes," I assured him. "I heard you."

"That was just for you, Dana," he told me. "You are a totally incredible actress. You should really think about going out for cheerleading."

"Cheerleading?" I repeated. Somehow I couldn't see myself ever being a cheerleader.

"Yeah, well, it's kind of the same thing," he said, leaning on me. "You know, you're out there in front of the crowd and everything."

"Oh," I said. "I get it."

Just then I felt someone behind me bend down and kiss my cheek.

"Michael," I said happily, turning around.

His arms were full of roses. He leaned forward to kiss me again and handed them to me.

"You were wonderful," he whispered in my ear.

"I'll leave you two lovebirds alone for a while," announced Bruce. He gave Michael a slap on the back. "You played a great game today, Tyler."

Michael grinned. "You, too, Bruce."

"It's going to be another great season for the Hornets," said Bruce with a grin. He winked at me. "You know you should think about that cheerleading thing, Dana. Really."

"Oh, sure, I will," I promised.

When he had gone, Michael turned to look at me. We both burst out laughing.

"What's going on? Are you actually planning on becoming a cheerleader?" he asked.

"Oh, sure, right away," I said sarcastically.

He shook his head. "I sure can't see you as one of those girls."

"Oh, some of them are okay," I said. "Kirsten is really nice." I paused. "Somehow I don't think

Cindy and I are ever going to be good friends, though.''

Michael smiled at me. "Do you know she's going out with Bruce now?" he asked.

"Really?" I said, surprised. "What happened to Ashley?"

Michael shook his head. "You know what Bruce is like."

"No, but I'm beginning to figure it out," I said, grinning. I looked around the room. "Well, this combination party idea seems to be going okay."

"Definitely," agreed Michael. "Hey, I even saw your friend Sophie sitting with Mark Rapetti. They seem to be hitting it off pretty well."

"You're kidding!" I said. I shook my head in amazement. "Who knows, maybe it'll become a tradition for the Hornets to go out with Drama Club girls instead of cheerleaders."

Michael laughed. "Where does that leave the cheerleaders?"

I shrugged. "Let them go out with the Drama Club guys."

He laughed again. "I don't know how well that would go over with your friend Carla, though."

He nodded toward the corner, where Carla and Bruce were standing together, talking. She looked like she was arguing about something, emphatically making her point and jabbing her finger in the air at him over and over. But Bruce didn't seem to be taking her seriously at all; he was just leaning back and grinning at her. The whole thing looked pretty funny, especially since Carla was about half Bruce's size.

"I hope she doesn't beat him up," joked Michael.

"He'd better watch out," I said. "Carla can be pretty tough."

We turned to each other and smiled.

I looked down at the roses in my arms. "Thank you for the flowers, Michael. They're beautiful."

"So are you," he said, gazing into my eyes.

We kissed.

"Listen, Dana," he said, "I wanted to ask you about something. You know, now that we've agreed to try to make plans together in advance and stuff from now on."

"Sure," I said. "What is it?"

He grinned. "What are you doing next summer?"

I grinned back. "I don't know. Why, Michael? Do you have something in mind?"

He nodded. "There's this great little lake I know. Not too exciting, not much to do, just walks and bike rides and ice cream cones and stuff. But I hear they might be looking for lifeguards."

"Oh, yeah?" I said. "Sounds interesting."

"Then it's a date?" he said, putting his arms around me again.

"Well," I said, gazing up into his eyes. "Maybe. But first I have to ask *you* something."

"What's that?" he asked.

I put my hand up to his head and rubbed his hair,

which was about three inches long now.

"Do you think this will have finished growing back by then?" I asked.

He laughed. "I sure hope so."

Award-winning author

NORMA FOX MAZER

MISSING PIECES
72289-5/$4.50 US/$5.99 Can

Jessie's father walked out on his family when she was just a baby. Why should sh care about him—it's clear he never cared about her. Yet after years of anxiety, a determined Jessie needs to know more about him, and over her mother's objections, Jessie decides to track him down.

DOWNTOWN
88534-4/$4.50 US/$5.99 Can

Sixteen-year-old Pete Greenwood is the son of fugitive radicals of the 1960's. Pete has been telling everyone that his parents are dead because it was easier than telling the truth. But when Pete meets Cary, someone he can really talk to, he wonders if he can trust her with his terrible secret.

And Don't Miss

OUT OF CONTROL	71347-0/$4.50 US/$5.99 Can
BABYFACE	75720-6/$4.50 US/$5.99 Can
SILVER	75026-0/$4.50 US/$5.99 Can
AFTER THE RAIN	75025-2/$4.50 US/$5.99 Can
TAKING TERRI MUELLER	79004-1/$4.50 US/$6.50 Can

Avon Flare Presents
Award-winning Author
JEAN THESMAN

MOLLY DONNELLY   72252-6/ $4.50 US/ $6.50 Can

On December 7, 1941, the Japanese bombed Pearl Harbor, and the world changed forever. It was the beginning of World War II and for Molly Donnelly, it was the end of childhood. But it was also a time of great discoveries—about first dates, first kisses, falling in love, and about all the wonderful possibilities that lay ahead when the war was over.

RACHEL CHANCE   71378-0/ $3.50 US/ $4.25 Can

THE RAIN CATCHERS

71711-5/ $4.50 US/ $5.99 Can

THE WHITNEY COUSINS: HEATHER

75869-5/ $2.95 US/ $3.50 Can

CATTAIL MOON   72504-5/ $4.50 US/ $5.99 Can